Murder Season in the Hamptons

Glowing Sands

Love

By:

Steven C. Drielak

Smith Creek

BARN

ISBN: 9781797637389

DEDICATION

To my wonderful grandson Chase.

CONTENTS

ACKNOWLEDGEMENTS

A great many thanks to Hampton Bays Historian Brenda St. Clair for her continued support in the historical research for this series of stories.

Prologue

Hampton Bays
Today

As Jake's eyes quickly scanned the open space around him, he saw the source of the odd glow. It was an old-fashioned oil lamp burning in the far corner of the barn. His eyes finally rested on what looked like an old rusted commercial van. The light was too poor to make out any of the writing on the panels and doors, but one of the doors looked like it had a big bell painted on the side. Both the back doors to the van were open. Jake stepped up to the back bumper and pulled his flashlight from his pocket. "Two seconds this time," he told himself. The powerful light beam lit up the inside of the van. There, up against the back wall that separated the cab from the cargo area, sat seven concrete casts.

The light suddenly changed from white to a blinding white heat. This was instantly followed by a pain so intense that it buckled Jake at his knees. By the time he hit the floor, he knew that he had been struck from behind. He tried to raise his body at his knees and reach for his Glock at the same time. Then a second blow came. It missed his skull by a fraction of an inch, tore his right ear in half and fractured his collarbone. Jake fell back to the floor and rolled onto his back. There was no hope now of drawing his Glock. The entire right side of his body was now ablaze in pain. Now Jake could see his attacker's face looming above him, shining in the lamp light.

PART 1

June 1965

Chapter 1

Operation Apollo

Mossad Agent Rafi Eitan had been waiting and watching for over an hour. A light rain had begun to fall which caused him to keep his engine running so that he could run his windshield wipers. He didn't want to miss his signal. His rental car was tucked into a neat little parking space in the far corner of the employee parking lot of the Nuclear Materials and Equipment Corporation in Apollo, Pennsylvania. It was a Sunday evening and the plant was officially closed. The company was usually referred to as NUMEC and its specialty was creating Highly Enriched Uranium for nuclear bombs. The man parked next to him in the Bell Telephone Company van was Yoni Levy. They had worked together several times in the past.

Yoni actually worked for LEKEM which was the Israeli intelligence agency and the van he was driving didn't really belong to Bell Telephone. Yoni had purchased it from a used car lot 10 days ago. The van was repainted and now included the familiar Bell Telephone logos on all sides of the van. Yoni had gone so far as to visit a Bell Telephone vehicle storage area late one evening just east of Pittsburgh. Once over the fence he found several Bell vans that had been badly damaged in accidents. They still had their license plates, however. Between the new paint job and plates registered to Bell Telephone, Yoni felt confident that he could drive that van on any road, park it anywhere and never arouse the slightest suspicion during his upcoming 435-mile journey to a little town on the eastern end of Long Island. Hiding in plain sight was one of Joni's specialties.

For this particular mission, he would need to bring all of his special skills to the table.

The owner of NUMEC was Zalman Shapiro. Zalman was world-renowned as a nuclear metallurgist. There was little he didn't know about uranium and plutonium. His true talent however, which he had honed in the US Navy's nuclear submarine development program, was the packaging of special nuclear materials so that they could be used in nuclear reactors, and in other things. Zalman Shapiro, owner of NUMEC, was also good friends with Yen Bergmann, Chairman of the Israeli Atomic Energy Commission and father of the Israeli atomic bomb development program.

Zalman had been producing highly enriched weapons-grade uranium for the US government for several years. A simple adjustment in the production records and a reliance on claimed accounting errors had allowed him to literally siphon off over 200 pounds of what many considered to be the most valuable metal in existence.

Rafi had met with Zalman just the day before to finalize the secret delivery of 206 pounds of weapons-grade Highly Enriched Uranium to the Israeli government.

This was just one of many such operations being conducted throughout the world by the Israeli security and intelligence services. The Israeli government truly believed that they would not survive as either a nation or a people if they could not obtain nuclear weapons to defend themselves. Building the bombs was not the issue. They had the technical ability and manufacturing facilities to build numerous bombs. Their real problem was obtaining the Highly Enriched Uranium necessary to fuel the bombs. They had very little of it and needed a great deal more.

This transaction with NUMEC was totally illegal of course. Had the FBI gotten wind of what was about to occur, Rafi's yearlong planning and hundreds of thousands of dollars would have been wasted on what many inside the Israeli Knesset would have considered an unacceptable risk.

Rafi checked his watch for the tenth time within the last 5 minutes. It was now 8:50 pm and the rain began to fall harder. As per his agreement with Zalman, the lights to the NUMEC loading bay would be turned on between 8:45 pm and 9:00 pm. Once the lights to the loading bay were turned on, Yoni would back the Bell Telephone Company van into loading bay number one, open the van's rear doors and then return to the driver's seat of the van. The cargo would be loaded by a forklift operator. The forklift operator would then hit the lock buttons and close the rear doors to the van. He would then signal Yoni that he could leave.

As Rafi sat watching the loading bay he had that sense of déjà vu. Just six years earlier he had been on another clandestine mission, one that had him sitting in a vehicle parked on the side of a dirt road in Buenos Aires, Argentina. He could still recall the sound of the rain that night landing on the roof of his car. He, along with several other Mossad agents, were all waiting on the side of Garibaldi Street for one of the world's greatest monsters to step off a municipal bus. The monster's name was Adolf Eichmann. Rafi hoped that this operation would be as successful as that one had been.

As Rafi sat in the NUMEC parking lot reliving his past, NUMEC employee Chet Morgan was climbing onto his forklift inside the plant. He was not a happy man. He had awakened this morning with a bad hangover and that was the bright spot of his day. First, it was supposed to be his day off, but Mr. Shapiro had called him in the middle of his Sunday family dinner.

Well, it wasn't really a family dinner. It was just him and his dog Kittie. Kittie was a stray that had showed up at his trailer's door one day a few years back. One free meal was all it took and old Kittie became Chet's new and only friend.

Chet liked to tell anyone who would listen that he purposely named his dog Kittie so that when he called his dog he could say, "Here Kittie, Kittie." He thought it was hilarious. The rest of the world thought it was stupid.

As Chet thought about Mr. Shapiro's call a little more, he realized he wasn't really eating dinner when the phone rang. But he was just about to crack open his third six-pack of beer. These days the beer usually served as his dinner.

Settling into the seat of the forklift, he thought to himself, "It's nobody's business what I eat or drink for dinner. Besides, it's supposed to be my day off."

Mr. Shapiro had told him on the phone that the foreman was supposed to do a two-hour job at the plant this evening, but he had slipped on some ice that day and might have broken his arm. On the bright side, Mr. Shapiro did tell him he would be getting overtime pay. He could always use a few extra dollars in his pocket.

The second thing that had ruined his day was his precious Philadelphia Eagles. They had just lost their fourth game in a row due to the stupidity of their idiot coach Joe Kuharich. The earlier realization that afternoon that there would be no playoffs this year for him and his team set him off on one of his famous drinking binges. Things were just beginning to look a little brighter when Mr. Shapiro called and spoiled what could have been one hell of an evening in the trailer.

Chet took a deep breath and reached for the starter button on his forklift.

At that moment a wave of nausea hit him hard. He knew he would never make it to the toilet. He just leaned over the side of the forklift and vomited all over the floor. He rested his head on the steering wheel for a moment. He needed both the pain and the spinning in his head to calm down before he could even think about moving again.

Chet sat there and decided to go over Mr. Shapiro's instructions one more time. He had already obtained the special storage area master key from Shapiro's office. It was hidden under the water cooler next to the old rolltop desk. He had then left the office suite area and headed to the far side of the plant. Using his master key he entered the special storage area and unlocked the large steel rollup door for room number one just as he had been told to do. In the three years that he had worked at NUMEC, he had never been allowed on this side of the plant. He wasn't really sure what was in the special storage area. Someone on the safety staff may have told him once, but he just could not remember the details.

He reached into storage room number one and flipped the light switch on the wall. When the room lit up he could see that it was a room approximately twenty feet by twenty feet. The walls, floor and ceiling were all made of thick poured concrete. In the middle of the room sat two thick wooden pallets, each holding four concrete casts.

Each cast was two feet high and one foot wide. The lid to each cast was also made of concrete and had an iron ring embedded in the top. Each concrete cast had a series of black numbers and letters stenciled on its side, along with the familiar yellow radiation symbol.

Now all he had to do was get his forklift and move both pallets to the loading bay door. Once that was done, his instructions were to turn on the loading dock lights, wait for a truck to appear and then move the pallets into the truck. If it weren't for the vomiting and growing pain in his head, he would normally have no problem with any of this.

Chet slowly lifted his head from the steering wheel and noted that the room had stopped spinning. He reached down and hit the starter button for the forklift. He moved his machine into the main hallway of the special storage area and slowly maneuvered the forklift into room number one.

All went well at first. He had successfully moved the first pallet to the loading bay door and had only stopped to vomit once. He now had the second pallet on the forklift and was backing out of room number one when things started to go bad.

First, he misjudged this turn and the front of the forklift struck the concrete-encased metal door frame. The force of the blow knocked one of the casts off the pallet. It hit the floor hard, fell over on its side and rolled for about two feet. Then its concrete lid fell off. Chet stopped the forklift and sat there staring at the floor trying to calculate how much trouble he was in.

Rafi was beginning to worry now. It was now 9:05 pm and the rear loading area of the plant still remained dark. He was sure that Yoni was also beginning to feel uneasy. He decided that he would give it just another few minutes and then he would signal Yoni to abort the mission.

Chet was just sober enough to know that he had to find some way to fix this situation and fix it fast. When he got off the forklift to examine the fallen cast, he saw that two large cracks had appeared on the side of the cast. Both cracks went from top to bottom.

He then lifted his head and looked down the hall at storage room number two. An idea began to emerge from his alcohol-induced stupor and he reached into his pocket for the master key. He unlocked storage room number two's rollup door and gave it a hard push upwards. Once it opened, he reached in and flipped on the light switch. Storage room number two was an exact duplicate of storage room number one with the exception that it was completely empty.

He decided to try storage room number three. When the overhead lights lit up the room he saw three concrete casts that looked exactly like the ones he had just moved, sitting on the floor in the far corner of the room. He went back to his forklift and slowly guided it into room number three. It took every ounce of his strength to pick up one of the 65-pound concrete casts and place it in the empty spot on the forklift's pallet that had been recently vacated by the broken cast.

Had Chet bothered to compare the writing stenciled on the side of his new passenger, he would have noted that it was different than the writing on all of the other casts he had picked up.

The other casts all had "^{235}U" stenciled on their sides. His new passenger had "^{60}CO" stenciled on its side. Another fact that Chet was completely unaware of was that this particular concrete cast had its interior lined with lead.

When it comes to radiological isotopes there are two kinds: dangerous and really dangerous. ^{235}U is uranium in its highly enriched form. It is a greyish metal that emits alpha particles. Alpha particles do not travel very far and will not penetrate the skin. The only real radiation danger occurs when uranium dust is inhaled into the lungs or if the uranium enters the digestive track. ^{60}CO is also known as Cobalt-60 and it is a completely different beast. It produces deadly gamma rays and needs to be heavily shielded at all times. This particular isotope can cause serious injury or even death after just a few minutes of continuous exposure.

NUMEC did not normally maintain a stock of Cobalt-60 at its facility. However, there had been a great deal of recent discussion with their Pentagon counterparts regarding the feasibility of creating a "dirty bomb" which would require just this type of isotope. In response to these discussions, NUMEC had acquired this mass quantity of Cobalt-60 from over 30 different suppliers in anticipation of a major classified government contract to produce the fuel for the new Cobalt bomb.

Rafi was now convinced that the operation had been compromised. He looked at his watch one last time and saw that it read 9:30 pm. He rolled down his window and signaled Yoni to roll down his. Rafi leaned out of his window and said, "That's it, let's get out of here."

Just as Yoni was about to respond, the lights in the loading bay came on. Rafi looked at the lit loading bay and then again at Yoni and said, "Let's do this. But keep your engine running and if I flash my headlights you hit the accelerator just as hard as you can."

Yoni nodded and slowly drove his van across the parking lot towards the loading bay. As Yoni backed his van into the main loading bay he saw the large steel rollup door begin to rise slowly. He thought to himself, "This is it. There is going to be either a forklift or a bunch of FBI agents on the other side of that door."

To his relief he saw the wheels to a forklift begin to appear. Yoni got out of the van and opened the back doors. He then backed the van up the remaining four feet. The loading dock floor was six inches higher than the floor of the van. Under normal circumstances this wouldn't be a problem. But for the still inebriated and addle-brained Chet Morgan, it would prove to be just another "bad thing" that happened to him on his day off.

Chet successfully loaded the first pallet of casts onto the van. By extending the forklift's arms he was able to nudge the pallet right up against the wall separating the cab from the cargo area. With the next pallet, Chet moved the forklift forward but this time he failed to stop at the edge of the loading platform. The wheels of the machine went over the lip and dropped six inches onto the bed of the truck.

This caused three things to occur simultaneously. First, due to the weight of the forklift, the rear of the van sank even further away from the loading dock floor. Then, in the front of the van, Yoni's body was thrown upwards and he hit his head on the ceiling of the van's cab. He tried to see what was happening by looking through the small rectangular opening in the rear wall of the cab, but all he could see was the front lights of the forklift. The final thing to occur was that the four casts on the forklift pallet slipped off their pallet and slammed into the four casts already in the van.

The effect was like a bowling ball hitting pins. The four casts on the floor of the van were hit with such force and at such an angle that they were rocked back and forth. Two of the casts fell over. One of the fallen cast's concrete lids slipped off and some of its 25 pounds of a greyish metal spilled onto the floor of the van. Stenciled on the side of that cast was "^{60}CO."

Chet immediately put his machine into reverse and managed to get all four wheels back onto the loading dock floor. He yelled to the van driver, "Everything is okay! Just pull the van up a few feet and I'll close the doors."

Yoni replied, "All right," and moved the van a few feet forward. He heard the pushbutton locks on the van's rear doors being depressed and both doors being slammed shut.

Chet Morgan yelled, "Go!" and Yoni pulled the van out of the loading bay.

From Rafi's point of view, all seemed to go as planned. He did see the van rock up and down a little, but it did not seem to affect the operation. What he didn't see was a swarm of FBI agents and uniformed policemen. This made him very happy.

As Yoni's Bell Telephone Company van passed his parked car, they simply nodded to each other. It was one of those "see you next time my friend" kind of nods. Neither knew that they would never see each other again.

Rafi pulled his rental car out of the NUMEC parking lot and headed for the Philadelphia airport. His role in this operation was now complete and he looked forward to his long and peaceful plane ride back to his office in Dimona.

Chet Morgan was still in the loading bay. He sat down on top of an old packing crate and was trying to get straight in his mind what he had to do next. Most of the nausea was gone and the pain in his head had shrunk down to a dull throb. He knew there was a lot of stuff he had to clean up inside the plant before the early morning shift showed up for work. What he didn't know was that his 3 minute exposure to the spilled Cobal-60 would kill him within 2 weeks. It would be a hard and painful death.

As Chet sat on the old packing crate his thoughts kept turning back to his emergency six pack sitting in a cooler in the trunk of his car. Finally he stood up and said out loud, "Screw it, it's my day off!" and reached into his pocket for his car keys.

Chapter 2

The Mission

Yoni Levy's drive through Pennsylvania had been uneventful. All had gone well until he reached the George Washington Bridge, where a tractor trailer carrying tires and a Volkswagen minibus painted in psychedelic colors had tried to occupy the exact same space, at the exact same time, in the middle of the bridge. This resulted in wreckage from the minibus spread over a quarter mile and caused the complete closure of the eastbound bridge lanes, which added an additional three hours to his planned seven-hour drive.

As Yoni's Bell Telephone Company van sat in a six-mile-long line of unmoving vehicles he thought about his older brother Zachery. It had been a number of years since he had seen him. The last time they spoken face-to-face had been in Jerusalem in 1949. They had fought side-by-side in the Battle of Jerusalem during the 1948 Arab-Israeli war. Both had received minor wounds, Yoni's the result of artillery fire from the attacking Jordanian forces, Zachery's the result of being hit in the leg by a sniper bullet.

After the war Yoni had decided that he was going to help build his new nation and eventually ended up in the intelligence service. Zachery wanted a new life and he wanted that new life to begin in America.

As cars around him began to slowly inch forward, Yoni thought about how much he was looking forward to meeting Zachery's American wife Annie and their five-year-old daughter Rachel. Although Yoni had not seen his brother in many years, they had always stayed in contact. There had been several personal letters back and forth each year as well as several hand-delivered letters courtesy of certain employees working within the Israeli UN delegation in New York City. The hand-delivered letters, initiated by Yoni, had begun to arrive at Zachery's home about a year ago. All of these letters involved Yoni's current mission.

Yoni's role in Operation Apollo was to ensure that the 206 pounds of Highly Enriched Uranium, so critical to his nation's survival, would arrive safety in Dimona, Israel. To this end, he had reached out to Zachery.

Three months prior they had agreed upon a final plan. Zachery, for his own safety, would never be told what his brother was bringing with him. All he was aware of was that his brother would arrive on a certain date and would need a garage or barn to park a truck in for several days.

After several days, he was told, some men would arrive to offload the truck and move its cargo to a new location. Yoni would supervise this operation and once the cargo was gone, Yoni would leave in the truck he arrived in.

Zachery suspected guns or munitions of some kind would be part of the cargo, but he kept his suspicions to himself.

In Yoni's mind, it was a relatively simple plan. He was to arrive at his brother's home on Mill Race Road in a coastal Long Island town called Hampton Bays. The home itself was close to the water and was located in a section of the town known as Springville. His brother's house was just 300 yards away from Smith Creek. The creek fed into Shinnecock Bay, which had an inlet that allowed quick access to the Atlantic.

The plan was for a fishing boat to land on the shore of Smith Creek where a team of Israelis would disembark. They would secure the cargo from Yoni's van, hidden in a barn on his brother's property. They would then move the cargo to their fishing boat and head for Shinnecock Inlet.

Once in the ocean they would travel 10 miles due south where they would rendezvous with an Israeli freighter bound for Cyprus, and the cargo would be transferred to the freighter.

Once the freighter reached the eastern Mediterranean, the freighter's captain would divert the vessel to the Israeli port of Ashdod. From there, Yoni's cargo would travel by truck to a special storage facility in Dimona.

While this was all happening, Yoni would leave his brother's home in the Bell Telephone Company van and drive to Kennedy Airport in New York City. He would wipe down the entire interior of the van and abandon it in the Pan American Airways parking lot. He would then begin his air travel home. Yoni planned on being present at Dimona when his cargo arrived.

Chapter 3

Hampton Bays

Yoni had now been inside the van for 9 hours.

Other than two quick stops for gasoline and some aspirin, he had never left the driver's seat. He traveled east along the Long Island Expressway to where it ended in a town known as Riverhead. From there he followed the signs for Hampton Bays.

As Yoni approached a traffic light at the intersection of Montauk Highway, he noted a diner directly across from him. It was the typical American dinner with its bullet shape and silver skin. He thought that the diner would be a good place to make his call from. He was to wait for 24 hours before he made his call to his contact at the Israeli delegation's offices in New York City.

It had been agreed that the 24-hour period would be used to monitor any FBI or local police activity that would indicate their awareness of the theft from NUMEC. The plan was for Yoni to make his call this day at exactly 9:00 pm.

If Yoni failed to make the call, all individuals working on Operation Apollo would immediately leave the country. Once Yoni made contact, the individual on the other end of the call would alert the crew of the fishing boat which would arrive at Smith Creek at 3:00 am the following morning.

As the traffic light in front of him changed from red to green, Yoni made a left onto Montauk Highway and headed east. Yoni loved these typical American small towns. He passed the usual church and a cemetery named Goodground. He thought to himself; "What a nice name for one's final resting place."

In the center of town he stopped at another traffic light. A quick survey of the businesses around him showed him a bar called the Rod & Reel and an appliance store on the far corner of the intersection called Suffolk Refrigeration. When the light turned green Yoni made a right-hand turn onto a road named Ponquogue and headed south. He passed a red brick school house on his right and eventually reached the end of Ponquogue.

A quick right and a left and Yoni found himself on Mill Race Road. He stopped and rolled down his window. He took a deep breath and could smell the salt from the ocean in the air. It was now 8:00 am.

Yoni still felt confident that no one would think twice about seeing a Bell Telephone Company van traveling down a rural street in a quiet little coastal town like Hampton Bays. Yoni drove slowly down Mill Race Road and immediately spotted his brother's barn. He turned into the dirt driveway which led to the barn's already opened doors, drove straight into the barn and shut off the engine.

He grabbed his small travel bag from the passenger's seat and stepped out of the van. As he stretched his legs and arms his right hand went reflexively to the back of his head. For some reason his movements had caused the pain from his low-grade headache to triple in intensity.

He shook off the pain the best that he could and looked around the barn. There were several shutters that were locked from the inside along with a small side door that was locked from the inside with an old-fashioned wooden bar stretching across the width of the door.

Yoni locked the cab's door, checked the locks on the rear of the van and walked out of the barn. As he was reaching for the swinging barn door, he saw Zachery appear from around the side of the barn. Both men smiled and reached out their arms at the same time. For one brief moment Yoni completely forgot about the pounding inside his head.

As Zachery and Yoni were about to step into the doorway of the house, Zachery reached out and placed a hand on his brother's shoulder. As Yoni turned towards him Zachery nodded in a southerly direction and said, "See that marsh and the patch of blue water just past it? That's Smith Creek. There's a small dock there that they can tie their boat up to. I'll walk you down there later if you want."

Yoni said, "Looks like about 300 yards from here."

Zachery nodded in agreement and reached to open the front door of his house. As they entered the foyer, they were met by Zachery's wife Anne and his daughter Rachel.

Rachel was 10 years old and appeared to be a miniature version of her mother. Both had long raven colored hair and big blue eyes. Anne was the daughter of a newspaper editor in New York City. She and her family had lived in the Gramercy Park section of Manhattan. She and Zachery had met in an accounting course at Baruch College, where both were studying. One cup of coffee and three dates was all it took for them to realize that they wanted to be together forever. They graduated from college, married and set up a small accounting firm in Southampton.

Rachel, an only child, was the center of Anne's and Zachery's lives. Yet although this could have made her spoiled, she was remarkably obedient as well as smart and pretty. She was simply a delightful child who did whatever she was told to do. She kept her room clean, herself clean and was always willing to lend a hand at whatever house or yard project needed to be done. She was also a very good student. At the last parent-teacher conference her sixth-grade teacher, Mr. Macaluso, had said she was the brightest student in his class and that they could expect great things from her in the future. It was no wonder that when she asked for a pet kitten she had one in her arms within a day, a white Persian she called Fluffy. Yoni, of course knew all of these things. Zachery had put them all into his many letters.

Anne immediately reached out her hand to Yoni and said, "Zack has been talking about you since the day I met him in New York City. It is wonderful to finally meet you in person."

Yoni replied, "You should know that every letter he sent to me in the last 11 years speaks about how lucky he is to have married someone like you." Yoni then turned his gaze to little Rachel and said, "...and you. I can't tell you how many times your dad told me in his letters that God had graced them with an angel. Now I know what he meant."

Rachel blushed and said, "Thank you, Uncle Yoni."

Anne quickly said, "You must be tired from driving." Pointing to her left she said, "We have a guest room ready for you down that hallway. There is also a connecting bath. If you're hungry, I'm about to put breakfast on the table."

Yoni smiled and said, "I think I will rest in my room for a little while."

To Zachery he said, "I think there may be something wrong with my van's engine. Would you be so kind as to give me a ride into town later this evening around 8:30? I have a short errand to run and it should not take long."

Zachery knew that his brother needed to make a call that evening and simply said, "Sure, no problem."

Yoni picked up his travel bag and headed for the guest room. Once inside, he shut the door and dropped his bag to the floor. He then headed straight for the toilet. He had been suppressing a wave of nausea since he entered the house. Kneeling in front of the porcelain bowl he emptied the contents of his stomach. He had eaten nothing that day and all that came out of his empty stomach was a lot of water. His head hurt horribly and he felt as if he had a fever coming on. He convinced himself that he had somehow contracted the flu and would need to stay clear of this brother's family. He slowly raised himself off the floor and walked into the bedroom.

He fell forward onto the bed, breaking through the shaft of dust-filled sunlight that was shining through the small window above his bed. He would remember nothing after that until he heard a slight tapping at his bedroom door.

Chapter 4

The Death Toll Begins

When Yoni's eyes opened, he felt that momentary sense of confusion that sometimes arrives with a sudden awakening.

What really threw him was the darkness of the room. He clearly remembered the sunlit window above his bed. Now the room was filled with nothing but dark shadows.

There was another tap at the door and the sound of his brother's voice saying, "Yoni, it's time for your errand." Yoni glanced at the luminous dial of his watch saw that it was 8:15 pm.

"Ok, give me five minutes," he said.

He went into the bathroom and turned on the cold-water tap. He drenched his face for a full minute. He reached for a towel and looked at his face in the mirror over the sink. He looked pale and gaunt. Both of his eyes were bloodshot and he was sweating profusely. He was also incredibly thirsty. But although the nausea had subsided, he did not want to risk another vomiting episode. He needed to be able to meet the fishing boat at 3:00 am and then drive himself to Kennedy Airport. Eight hours was all he needed. He decided to rinse his mouth with cold water and take a small sip.

He promised himself a tall glass of ice water when he returned from making his call.

Zachery waited in his car while Yoni climbed the front steps of the Hampton Bays Diner. Zachery knew that something was wrong with his brother but he also knew it would have to wait until Yoni's mission was complete.

Yoni slid into one of the wooden phone booths in the rear of the diner. He sat there staring at his watch. At exactly 9:00 pm, he dialed his New York City contact's number. The operator came on the line and told him to deposit seventy-five cents for the first three minutes. The phone on the other end of Yoni's call only rang once before the receiver was picked up.

A female voice at the other end of the line began talking immediately. She said in a quiet but firm voice, "The timetable has been pushed back exactly 24 hours due to weather. Repeat the verification procedure tomorrow."

With that the line went dead. Yoni had not uttered a single word. He stared at the phone in his hand for a moment and went over in his head what he had just been told. What weather could she have been talking about?

Yoni had not listened to any type of news for at least two days. The radio antenna on his van had been broken off and the radio failed to function. It was one of the reasons he got the van so cheaply at the used car lot in Pennsylvania.

Unbeknownst to Yoni a hurricane named Alma was moving up the east coast. Hurricane Alma had developed in early June over Central America and slowly moved through the Gulf of Mexico towards Key West. Its winds had been clocked at 125 mph. Alma had moved north the previous day and crossed into Georgia as a tropical storm. The storm re-intensified into a hurricane over the western Atlantic, and its outer rain bands would be dropping heavy rainfall and winds along the southern coast of Long Island. Clearly not ideal weather conditions for transferring Highly Enriched Uranium from one boat to another at sea.

Yoni left the phone booth and headed for the door of the diner. He suddenly stopped, turned and ran towards the sign that said "Men's Room." Ten minutes later, Yoni climbed into the front passenger seat of Zachery's car. Without saying a word, Zachery backed out of the parking space and headed east on Montauk Highway.

"There's been a delay," said Yoni in a raspy and stunted voice. "Twenty-four hours. I think there may be a storm coming up the coast."

Zachery could see that sweat was pouring off his brother's forehead and his left hand was visibly trembling. "You need to see a doctor."

"No," replied Yoni, "not until it's gone."

They drove in silence for a few more minutes. Suddenly Yoni said, "Pull the car over quick."

Zachery did as he was told and pulled the car under a street lamp. He watched his brother leap from the car and heard sound of his brother's retching. Zachery threw the car into "Park" and got out. He circled around behind the car and knelt down next to his brother. Yoni was lying in a fetal position on the ground, holding his stomach. There was blood on the ground and on Yoni's mouth.

Zachery spoke softly. "What is it, Yoni? What's wrong with you?"

"I don't know," said Yoni. "I just don't know."

Zachery lifted his brother up and placed him in the passenger seat. He got into the car and headed for home.

When Zachery arrived home he could see that all of the lights were off in the house. That was a good sign. It meant that both Anne and Rachel had gone to bed early. Now all he had to do was get Yoni into his room. He would call Doctor Saffer in the morning and arrange to get Yoni examined. Zachery circled the car and opened the passenger door.

Yoni was slumped over in his seat. He breathing was heavily labored and his eyes appeared to be glued shut. As Zachery put his arms around Yoni's chest to lift him he saw Yoni's eyes flicker open. They stared at each other for a moment.

Yoni spoke softly in a voice that rang of finality. "I love you, Zack." He then said, "Watch over the van for me. Someone will reach out to you."

Zachery looked down at his brother's face and said, "Hey, you're gonna be..." But before he could finish his sentence, Yoni's eyes rolled up into his head and the noises emanating from his chest ceased.

Zachery, as a younger man at war, had seen death many times and he knew that his brother was gone.

It was now midnight. Zachery sat on the ground next to the lifeless body of his brother. He had been sitting on the ground for close to two hours. The tears were now gone and he knew what he had to do. But, as with many things in life, the first step would be the hardest. For him, it meant going into the house to pack up Yoni's things and then getting a shovel from his shed. But the first thing he had to do was just stand up.

Three hours later, Zachery stood over the unmarked grave of his brother Yoni. He had buried him next to a large oak tree 100 yards south of his house.

He picked this spot on purpose. Now, whenever he looked out of his kitchen window he would see both Yoni's grave and the deep blue water of Smith Creek.

The next morning Zachery told the one and only lie to his wife that he would ever tell. He told her that Yoni had been recalled by his employer and had taken an early train to New York City and that he would contact them when he could. After breakfast that morning he asked Rachel to come to the barn with him. They stopped about twenty feet from the barn and Zachery knelt and faced his daughter.

He said, "Rachel, I want you to listen to me carefully. Uncle Yoni left a few of his things in the barn. I am going to lock it up tight until it's time to return those things. You are never to go in there under any circumstances." He continued, "You need to promise me."

She replied, "I promise, daddy." She then looked at him and asked, "Daddy, will I ever see Uncle Yoni again?"

Zachery thought for a moment and said, "Yes, Rachel, we will all see him again."

No one ever contacted Zachery Levy regarding the contents of the Bell Telephone van parked in his barn and Rachel, being the good girl that she was, kept the promise she had made to her father that morning.

PART 2

August, 1977

Chapter 5

Zachery Tells All

Rachel Levy sat on the front porch of her family's home on Mill Race Road. It was late afternoon and the sun was just beginning to sink below the horizon. She was thinking about all that had happened to her in the past couple of years, especially the loss of both her parents.

Her mother, Anne, went first. It was a simple and sudden heart attack that happened on a Saturday afternoon right in the middle of Thompson's Supermarket. An off-duty policeman was in the store at the time and did CPR on her until the volunteer ambulance arrived but she was dead by the time she reached Southampton Hospital.

Her father lasted another year. It was a blood clot in the lung that took him.

Up until then it seemed the perfect life for Rachel. She had fond memories of growing up in Hampton Bays. As far as she was concerned her time in high school would always remain a highlight in her life. She remembered her first kiss. It happened behind one of the temporary classrooms that had been built behind the cafeteria. There had been a dance in the cafeteria that evening and she and her first boyfriend had stepped out for some fresh air.

She remembered when, a year or two later, she had pleaded with her guidance counselor Mr. Brown to allow her to take wood shop. She argued that she had straight "A"s and a free period. She had told him and the Industrial Arts teacher Mr. Maginski that she wanted to learn how to build furniture and perhaps open her own furniture store in town someday. The real reason she wanted to take wood shop was because Billy Paxton was in that class. He was seventeen and the Captain of everything. He was also as dumb as a box of rocks. But boy, was he ever pretty.

There were the Friday night basketball games, cheerleading and, of course, the senior prom that had been held at the Canoe Place Inn and it could not have been more perfect. Her parents had even bought her a used car as a graduation present. The car was a used 1970 Fiat Spider convertible painted in British Racing Green and it was just plain fun to drive.

She had decided to go to college locally. She had spent much of her time growing up working and playing on the waters surrounding Hampton Bays. She had worked as the first mate on a local fishing boat and had sat many hours in the lifeguard's stand at Ponquogue Beach. She had always been fascinated with the many different forms of sea life that thrived in these waters and the landscapes that surrounded those waters. While in college she had taken a painting course and found she had a knack for painting beaches, sunsets and sea birds. All of these related interests moved her towards an interest in marine biology, which turned out to be her major at Southampton College.

She was just beginning her third year at the college when her mother passed. She had just begun her fourth year when her father died. She and her dad had been very close and she found her sense of loss overwhelming at times.

She thought that he must have had some sense that his time was coming near. Just a month before he died, he had asked her to join him at the kitchen table. He had one of his accounting business folders in front of him. She remembered him tapping the folder with his finger and saying, "This folder contains my signed and notarized Will along with a list of all my assets. I keep it in my desk in the study. There is no mortgage on this property and I suggest you eventually sell this house after I am gone. This house requires a great deal of maintenance and will quickly begin to deteriorate if the upkeep is not maintained. You could easily buy something smaller that would require fewer repairs."

He continued, "Even though that all makes perfect business sense, you cannot sell the house or even rent it to anyone after I am gone. At least not right away." She simply stared at her father. She did not want to have this conversation or even think about losing her only remaining family member. "Rachel! This is important and I need you to tell me that you understand what I am telling you." Rachel dropped her eyes to the floor and nodded her head.

"Rachel, please look at me," he said in a much softer voice. "There is one other thing," he said. "Do you remember your Uncle Yoni…?"

She had remembered her Uncle Yoni that day at the kitchen table, and she had been reminded of him again today when she had gotten a phone call that morning.

Chapter 6

All Roads Lead East

As Rachel sat on her porch thinking about her life, a man named Aharon Kagan was picking up a rental car at Newark Airport. Aharon Kagan wasn't his real name of course. But that is what it said on his passport and it would suffice for the purposes of this mission. He had just arrived that morning from a multi-stopover flight that landed him in six different countries. His original point of departure had been Tel Aviv. His final destination was a small coastal town on the eastern end of Long Island.

...

That same morning, a twenty-four-year-old young man named Richard Falco was heading eastbound on the Long Island Expressway. He was driving his yellow 1970 Ford Galaxie. Richard Falco had just recently become aware of his name. It seems that, according to the Adoptee's Liberty Movement Association in New York City, his real parents were named Betty and Tony Falco and they hailed from Brooklyn. He now had a copy of his original birth certificate in his pocket. It seems his adoptive parents, good ole Nathan and Pearl, had failed to mention this minor fact about his newfound heritage for 24 years. He had been quite stressed out about this and had missed several days of work. During the prior evening a very imposing acquaintance of his had told him that he should visit, for therapeutic reasons, the Hamptons and perhaps visit some of the places he had visited as a child. So, early this morning, the new Richard Falco had put on his bathing suit under his denim shorts, packed an overnight bag and headed for Long Island.

As Richard guided his big Ford down the Long Island Expressway he kept checking his speedometer. The last thing he wanted to do was to draw the attention of any over-achiever policeman types. If he did, he knew it wouldn't go very well. He still maintained a vivid memory of his adoptive father Nathan being pulled over on this very road many years ago and being handed a handful of tickets. Richard had decided that he wanted to take the same route he had taken as a child and ended up winding his way through Riverhead and a little town called Flanders.

What he really wanted to do was to see if "it" was still there. He remembered being mesmerized by its very sight and size as a child. "It" was a giant duck.

Not a big duck. A giant duck, the size of a small building. It was painted bright white with a giant orange bill. As he traveled down Flanders Road towards Hampton Bays his eyes swept from the right side of the road to the left until finally he saw it in the distance. He slowed and turned into the Duck's parking lot. In the back of his mind he knew he had places to go and important things to do, but he just had to do this. He parked his car, got out and walked to the very side of the building.

He placed his hands on the bright white wall, closed his eyes and whispered the word, "Magnificent."

...

Eight-year-old Betsy Vail watched from her yard as Miss Rachel, as she liked to call her, pulled out of her driveway in her green sports car. She always liked the way Miss Rachel would wave at her whenever she passed her in the street. Most times it was when Betsy was riding her bike. She was allowed to ride her bike around the neighborhood but was not allowed to ride it on Springville Road which was the big road. She lived with her parents in a house on Oak Lane which was right around the corner from Miss Rachel's House. As a matter of fact, Betsy's backyard backed right up to Miss Rachel's property.

Betsy was especially excited today because she had recently made a new friend. It was a big fat calico cat that had been visiting her back door for the past two weeks.

Betsy had been feeding the calico a saucer of milk every day and three days ago the cat had actually crawled up into her lap. Betsy decided to name her new friend Sir Lancelot and she was determined to find out where the cat lived.

The last two times she tried to follow the cat it had gone into the marshy area over by Smith Creek. Betsy followed the cat as far as she could before the ground became real squishy. She knew what that meant and had learned her lesson last year when she sank right up to her knees into the mud. She managed to get out, but her right shoe didn't. Her mother was not happy to find her crying on the front porch, covered in mud and missing a shoe.

Today, however, was different. Sir Lancelot had finished the saucer of milk, spent the obligatory time on Betsy's lap and then took off at a run. This time Sir Lancelot ran across Betsy's backyard and headed for Miss Rachel's old red barn. The cat then disappeared around one of the corners. By the time Betsy got to the corner of the barn, Sir Lancelot had disappeared.

As Betsy moved along the side of the barn, she saw a hole in the wall large enough for Sir Lancelot to have slipped through. She saw that two of the big boards that made up the barn's siding had come loose. One of the boards looked like it might fall off at any second. Betsy crouched down and looked into the crack between the boards. There was some light inside the barn and she could see the tires of a car. She pulled her head back and thought to herself, "How can there be any light in there? All the windows are boarded up."

She leaned forward again and called into the crack, "Sir Lancelot! Are you in there?"

She pulled her head back again and tried to decide what to do. She thought that she might be able to move the loose board a little more so that she could squeeze through. Then she thought that she might get into trouble for going into the neighbor's barn. As she stood up to leave, she heard it. It was a simple "meow" which came from the hole in the wall.

That was all it took. In her eight-year-old mind, the "meow" was a cry for help.

Betsy put both hands on the big loose board and pushed. The crack widened. Two more pushes and the crack was now wide enough for her to crawl through. Then there was another "meow." She went to her knees and yelled, "I'm coming! I'm coming!" She then crawled through the hole.

...

Richard had said goodbye to his giant duck friend and was now driving slowly down the main street in Hampton Bays. He had just passed the old Lyzon Hat Shop. He remembered when he and his adoptive mother visited the shop several times in the early 1960s. He thought he remembered reading a New York Times article recently about the owner, a Mr. King, passing away the previous year. The old hat shop was now empty and appeared to be in a major state of disrepair.

As he approached the heart of the little village he seemed to remember a restaurant along this section of town that he had eaten at as a child. Just before he came to the main intersection traffic light he spotted the place on the right hand side of the road. There was a simple sign above the door that said "Carolyn's Luncheonette."

He made a right hand turn at the light and spotted a Post Office a few hundred feet down the road. He pulled his Ford into the Post Office parking lot and got out. Looking around he spotted a small alleyway that led back out to the village's main street. Two minutes later he was sitting on an ancient chrome spinning stool with a red Naugahyde seat cushion. The long L-shaped counter in front of him was straight out of the 1950s and was complete with a set of chrome mixers used to make old-fashioned malted milk shakes. The place reminded him of the old Woolworth counters he had seen as a child. There was even a large mirror on every wall that made the place appear bigger than it actually was. Richard noted a thin dark-haired man working a grill right in front of where he was sitting. There was even a middle aged waitress with a pencil stuck in her hair bringing food to one of the booths. He spun around on his stool two full turns and came to a stop. Had anyone been watching him they would have seen a young man with a look of pure glee on his face. He snapped the small two-sided paper menu from the steel rack in front of him and started reading.

As he was trying to decide between the egg salad sandwich and the BLT, he heard the restaurant's door open behind him and he instinctively looked up into the big wall mirror behind the counter. What he saw caused him to feel as if a giant icicle had just pierced his chest. He became aware that he was no longer breathing. His eyes were frozen to the image in the mirror. Coming up right behind him and staring right at the back of his head was a uniformed cop.

As Richard's hand slid to his waistband he noted two things about this particular policeman. First, he had one of those big black Motorola portable radios in his hand. Second, this cop had to be the skinniest cop Richard had ever seen in his life. Just as Richard's hand reached his waistband his inner voice began to scream at him, "Do it now! Do it now!"

As he was spinning his body around on the stool and tugging at his waistband, he heard the policeman say, "Hi, Uncle Jimmy!" and then he sat down on the empty stool right next to Richard.

The man working the grill turned around, smiled and said, "Hey, Tommy! How's your day going?"

Richard slid off his stool and headed for the door.

...

Aharon Kagan was driving on Route 24 in a place called Flanders. He had just glanced at the map of Long Island that he had purchased when he stopped earlier for coffee. The map indicated that he should be entering Hampton Bays in just a few minutes.

Aharon kept his Pontiac LeMans moving just slightly over the speed limit. He still remembered the lecture from his training academy days on how to act when in America.

First, he was told, always look at pretty girls but never touch them. If you don't look at them, someone may think there is something wrong with you. If you touch them, then they will know for sure that there is something wrong with you. Second, driving too slow in America will draw the same kind of attention from a policeman as if you were driving too fast. Best to drive slightly over the speed limit as most Americans do.

Aharon had just passed one of the strangest sights he had ever seen. He was still shaking his head in disbelief as he approached the end of Route 24. He had just passed a building shaped like a giant white duck. It made him think that if his country could ever stop being at war, perhaps they could find the time to build whimsical buildings like the one he just saw, instead of the ever-growing number of bomb shelters.

It was now time for him to begin to think about the things he had to do before his flight out of JFK in the morning. He had to get a look at an old barn on Mill Race Road. He was to get pictures of the barn for the operational team if possible. He was also supposed to get a look at a Smith Creek and determine if a fishing boat would be able to land on the shore. He had no idea as to why a fishing boat might need to land there. In fact, he had no idea why the Mossad wanted pictures of the barn. All he knew was that he was to make contact with the Levy girl and let her know that the property that her uncle had left there many years ago was about to be retrieved. He, of course, had his suspicions about the mission. This kind of planning and the commitment of covert resources in a foreign country could only mean a high-ranking Nazi was about to be kidnapped or something of military value was about to be added to the Israeli arsenal. Since this was not South America, which was where most of the high-level Nazis had relocated, and since his country stood at the brink of war with seven Arab countries, he believed he was dealing with some type of military asset.

All this was simply conjecture on his part. He knew and accepted the rules regarding "operational security" and "the need to know."

Aharon had called the Levy girl the moment he landed and had told her he was an old friend of her Uncle Yoni and that he would be passing through town this evening and would love to meet her somewhere for a cup of coffee.

There had been a long silence on the other end of the phone and the Levy girl finally said, "Is this about my Uncle Yoni's property in the barn?"

Although Aharon had been taken aback by the abruptness of the question he quickly regained his composure and replied, "Yes, it is."

Surprising him again she said, "I don't know what is going on, but I suspect it may be best if no one ever sees us talking together. I know a secluded place in town that we can meet. Here are the directions..."

...

When Betsy entered the barn on her knees she ran face-first into a large spider web. She started furiously wiping her face with her hands and then started patting her clothes. Betsy had never been afraid of spiders. At least not until last year when she found out that her friend Cheryl Craft, who lived about a mile away, had been bitten by a Brown Recluse. Cheryl had been getting a rake for her father from the tool shed behind her house. She said her whole hand had turned black and hurt real bad. She had to stay in the hospital for four days. Her mom and dad had told her she would probably have the scar for her whole life.

Betsy stood up and checked the rest of her clothes and hair for spiders. When she was done, she lifted her gaze and studied her surroundings. The first thing that caught her attention was the sunlight that was pouring in through a hole in the roof. The hole was about the size of a football. She looked down and saw some of the roof's asphalt shingles on the barn floor along with a lot of scattered hay. Her eyes then rested on the only object she could see in the barn. It was a big van with the faded words "Bell Telephone" painted on the sides. It was covered with rust, dust and cobwebs and two of the tires looked flat. She walked slowly around the back of truck trying to find a window to peak into. As she moved around the truck, she thought to herself, "Why would Miss Rachel want to drive this creepy old truck when she has that neat sports car?"

She suddenly remembered why she was there. Her eyes swept across the floor and then moved to each corner of the barn. She called for the cat, "Sir Lancelot! Where are you?" She then heard another "meow." Sir Lancelot was close. She looked to her left and then to her right. Seeing nothing, she fell to her knees and peered under the truck.

"Oh my God! Kittens!" she yelled.

...

Richard was just beginning to calm down as he drove his Ford Galaxie over the old green iron bridge on the eastern side of town. He had just passed the old Canoe Place Inn and was now crossing over the Shinnecock Canal. To his left he spotted the old train bridge. He had spent many hours fishing off the bulkhead under that bridge. He crossed the bridge and traveled another quarter mile and saw his destination, the Hampton Maid, where he and his adoptive parents had vacationed for several summers when he was a little boy. He had remembered it as a little white motel located high up on a hill on the north side of Montauk Highway. What he remembered most of all were the owners, Jack and Marie Polanski. They lived in a house next to the motel and had three children of their own. There was a boy who was a year or two older than himself and two little girls. He suddenly remembered seeing the whole family coming and going in one of those red station wagons with what looked like wood paneling on its sides. He had a vivid memory of the girls playing on a swing set behind the motel. One memory then led to the next and he recalled that the motel office had one of those old ice coolers with the glass sliding top. It was always filled with little glass bottles of Coca Cola. The Cokes were ten cents each then and were always very cold.

As Richard stepped out of his car he marveled at how the place had changed. The little office was gone along with the long white building with side-by-side rooms. What he saw now was a modern multi-building hotel complete with a swimming pool and a cedar-shake-covered windmill. The windmill actually had guest rooms inside. He also noted that there was now a separate building which held the office, gift shop and restaurant. For a brief moment he thought that perhaps he was at the wrong place and that time had clouded his memory. Then he saw the big numbers "259" attached to the wall near the office entrance. He had remembered the address. This was the place he wanted to be regardless of what it looked like today.

Richard opened the red-painted screen door and stepped into the office. A middle-aged woman was standing behind the desk reading what looked like a menu. He was pretty sure she was one of the owners, Mrs. Polanski, but he was not positive. She stopped reading, looked up and smiled at Richard. Then he knew it was her. He remembered that smile. It was the one he had gotten every time he had come to the office to buy his bottle of Coca Cola. Richard smiled back and said in a cheery voice, "Hi, I'm Richard Falco. I have a reservation for this evening."

...

As Richard was filling out his room registration card just a few miles away, little Betsy Vail was trying desperately not to spill the bowl of milk she was carrying. After she had seen the kittens, she hurried home to get some milk for Sir Lancelot. As she was carrying the filled bowl across her back yard it occurred to her that she might need a new name for Sir Lancelot now that Sir Lancelot was a new mother. Betsy managed to avoid spilling any of the milk as she crawled through the opening in the barn wall for the second time that day. She sat down on the dusty floor next to the old truck and saw that Sir Lancelot was feeding four of her babies. The other two were sleeping next to each other. Betsy couldn't believe how tiny they were. She thought to herself that they must have just been born within the last day or two. She bent over and slid the bowl of milk under the truck and said to her calico friend, "You don't have to come to my house anymore. You can stay here with your babies and I will bring milk to you every day."

...

Richard finished checking in and drove his car around to the back of the building that contained his second-floor room. He had just opened his trunk and reached in for his overnight bag and his Long Island Rand McNally Road Atlas when he saw the long brown paper-wrapped package. He stared at it for a few moments and then thought to himself, "I'll need you later."

He then closed the Galaxie's trunk and climbed the stairs to his room. When he entered the room he threw his bag on the bed and headed for the bathroom. When he had finished relieving himself he went to the large window that faced south and looked out. There before him was a beautiful view of Shinnecock Bay. It was such a clear day that he could see all the way out to the barrier beach on the far side of the bay. He looked down and was again overwhelmed with memories. He saw the little white cottage that sat on the other side of Montauk Highway. There was a small cove that crept right up to the back door of the cottage. He remembered taking his toy soldiers down to the cove and floating them on a small raft along the shore line. He saw Pawnee Street that led directly to the bay. He used to walk down that street and look for Indians that might have been hiding in the tall reeds ready to swoop down on him. He remembered the rocky shore of the bay and that special smell that only existed at the shoreline.

Richard took a deep breath and then let it out slowly. It was time for him to get to work and fulfill his responsibility. He sat down at the small writing desk and placed the atlas in front of him. He thumbed through the pages and stopped when he got to the page that showed the south fork of Long Island and the little hamlet of Amagansett. The map showed that it was about 20 miles to the east. Now all he had to do was remember how to get to a place called Asparagus Beach.

Chapter 7

A Day at the Beach

Rachel sat at her kitchen table and looked up at the clock hanging above the refrigerator again. She still had a few hours to go and she didn't quite know what to do with herself. When the man had called this morning, he said his name was Aharon and that he was a friend of her Uncle Yoni. He said he wanted to talk to her about the property that Uncle Yoni had left in her barn over a decade ago. She could still remember her father kneeling down next to her when she was little and making her promise never to go into the barn, and later, the year he died, telling her that someone might reach out to her someday regarding Uncle Yoni. She remembered once trying to peek into a small crack in one of the wooden window shutters, but the barn had been dark inside and she could not make out anything at all. She had obeyed her father and now whatever it was that was so important would be going away.

It was a good thing that it was happening now she thought. The barn needed work. She thought she saw a cat go through a crack in the wall the other day. The real good news was that she had a plan for the barn. She thought that, with a little effort on her part, it would make a fine art studio.

...

Richard was traveling eastbound on Montauk Highway. He passed through the quaint little villages of Bridgehampton and East Hampton. He had heard that lots of movie stars and rich politicians had summer homes in these places. He passed farm stands, farm fields, war memorials, ponds and windmills. It all pretty much looked the same to him. He had only been down this highway once or twice when he was very young and had no real recollection of any of the sights.

Finally he entered the little hamlet of Amagansett. The main street was a quaint little village just like all the other quaint little villages along the south fork of Long Island. Its actual population during the non-summer months was under a thousand residents. That number quadrupled during the summer season, when the hamlet's 6.5 square miles of land and water became the favorite vacation spot for politicians, movie stars and millionaires. Richard had read somewhere that the area was named by the Montaukett Indians and referred to a "place of good water."

Richard drove slowly down the short main street and then, after another rural stretch of road, he saw what he was looking for. It was Atlantic Avenue. He made a right-hand turn off the highway and headed due south. After about a half mile he saw the parking lot for the beach.

Not just any beach. This was the famous Asparagus Beach where sun worshippers arrived for only two reasons. The first and most important reason was to meet and party with an attractive member of the opposite sex. In furtherance of this goal, just about every girl on this beach was attired in a string bikini. This beach had a long-standing reputation among the young people for being the place for fun, frolic and sex. The second reason young people came to this beach was to view the Hollywood celebrities who so often appeared. In fact, that is how the beach got its peculiar name. It seems that when a celebrity was seen coming onto the beach, everyone would get off their beach towels and blankets and stand up and stare. This happened all at once and the crowded beachgoers all ended up looking like stalks of asparagus.

Richard only remembered coming to this beach once or twice as a young boy with his adoptive father. But he had read recent articles about this particular beach. He knew that this was where he had to step up and fulfill his responsibility.

Richard parked his car next to a building called "The Hut." He grabbed a beach towel off the rear seat of his car and headed for one of the tall sand dunes. He looked at his watch and saw that it was a little after four o'clock in the afternoon. As he settled into his spot on top of the dune he took a long look at the mass of people in front of him.

He felt the usual rage begin to build inside of him. There they were in their skimpy little bathing suits doing their best to ruin the life of every young man on the beach. How he hated them all. He had promised to dedicate his life to stopping these creatures from hell. Taking them one-at-a-time would no longer satisfy him. Today, he was going to make a statement. Today, he was going to take bold action. It would be an action that the world, especially those fucked up newspaper people, would remember forever.

As he sat on his sand dune he did his best to ignore the evil filth that paraded up and down the beach in front of him. He turned from them and looked east across the dunes and suddenly remembered a story his adoptive father had told him many years ago about this very beach. His adoptive father was an amateur military historian and loved to talk about World War II and Hitler. They had been sitting close to this very spot and his adoptive father had pointed to the very same dunes that Richard was now looking at and said, "Just a little over 20 years ago, four Nazi sailors came ashore on this very patch of beach using a rubber boat that they paddled from a German submarine stationed just offshore."

It was sometime around midnight on June thirteenth, 1942. It was a dark night and the four Nazis had moved under the cover of a thick fog bank. Their rubber raft contained wooden boxes loaded with explosives, fuses, and timers. The boxes were sealed in wax to protect them from the salt. These four Nazi saboteurs' mission was to destroy bridges, factories, aluminum and magnesium plants, canals, locks, dams and anything else that they could that would hurt the American war effort. The saboteurs buried the boxes of explosives in the sand and intended to come back later for them.

Unfortunately for the Nazis, they were confronted by a 21-year-old Coast Guardsman by the name of John Cullen who was patrolling the beach. Cullen, who was unarmed, had just left the Atlantic Avenue Coast Guard Station to begin his beach patrol when he encountered the men on the beach just to the east of the station. The leader of the saboteurs was a man named George Dasch. Instead of killing John Cullen, Dasch offered him a bribe of $260 dollars to forget what he had seen. Cullen agreed, took the money and walked away. When he was finally out of sight of the saboteurs, he ran to the station and sounded the alarm. By the time the Coast Guardsmen returned to the beach, the saboteurs were gone. They did find the spot where the explosives had been buried and dug them up.

The saboteurs spent several hours hiding in the woods until finally they felt it was safe to walk to the Amagansett Railroad Station. They had boarded an early morning train and headed for Manhattan.

Richard tried to remember what happened to the Nazis after they got onto their train. He seemed to remember his adoptive father telling him that they were all eventually caught by the FBI and some of them had been executed.

Richard looked at his watch again. It was now six o'clock and he didn't have a clear recollection as to what he had just been thinking about. He looked around and realized he hadn't moved for two hours. As he looked across the growing throng of young people, he heard a rumble off in the distance. He looked to the western horizon and saw a pencil like line of dark clouds stretching from north to south.

Another trance-like muse and another look at his watch told him it was time to go to the trunk of his car. He could not put it off any longer. The rage that had been building since he arrived had now turned into a sense of clear-minded purpose. He had felt like this before and he knew exactly what he had to do.

As Richard got up and began walking toward his car, he noticed that the light was fading quickly. He was about halfway to the Galaxie when a bolt of lightning stretched across the sky right in front of him, followed by a rumbling that actually shook the sand at his feet. It wasn't thunder that he heard. It was the sound of golf-ball sized hailstones striking the metal roofs of the hundreds of cars in the parking lot.

As he ran for his car, he turned and looked behind him and saw hundreds of beach goers running for the shelter of their cars. He stopped dead in his tracks and fell to his knees.

His rage was in full bloom. He wanted to scream at them all to tell them to go back to beach. He *needed* them to go back. He raised his face to the now-jet-black sky above and screamed, "Noooo!"

To anyone who had been listening, it would have sounded more like a howl than a scream.

...

Little Betsy Vail was sitting in her favorite blue wing-backed chair in front of the TV set in her family's living room. The TV dinner her mother had made for her sat untouched next to her on a little table. Onscreen Paddington Bear was getting into hot water and lathering up a storm of suds, but Betsy wasn't enjoying his antics.

Tears were rolling down her face. She had just returned a little while ago from visiting Sir Lancelot and her new family in the barn. She had spent hours with her new friends today. When she had arrived in the barn that afternoon, she had discovered that two of the kittens were dead and that Sir Lancelot was not moving. Her calico friend was making really loud breathing noises like the kind you make when you have a really bad chest cold. She knew that there was something very wrong with her friends, and she had sat for a long time on the ground next to the van, reaching underneath to stroke the tip of one of Sir Lancelot's white paws. The cat didn't move, just kept breathing harshly as if she had a terrible chest cold.

Betsy reached for the paper napkin that sat next to her untouched dinner to wipe her face. As she dried her tears, a sudden wave of nausea made her leap from her chair and run for the bathroom.

Chapter 8

Death on the Canal

Richard pulled in behind his building at the Hampton Maid. The torrential downpours had become a light rain. As he climbed the steps towards his room, the same question kept repeating in his mind, "What am I going to tell him? What am I going to tell him?"

When he got into his room, he began to pace between the bed and his window. Finally, he stopped at the window and looked down at his childhood playground. He looked across the highway and saw the cove and the tall reeds along Pawnee. That is where he needed to be.

He checked his waistband, put on a lightweight jacket over his wet polo shirt and left his room. As he crossed the Hampton Maid's grounds he stopped at the little swing set that stood behind the restaurant. He grabbed one of the tall metal swing set legs, rested his head against the pole and rolled it back and forth across the cold metal. He knew that if was ever going to finish what he had to do, he needed to calm down.

He started down the steep drive of the Hampton Maid and got to the highway. He was about to cross the road when he suddenly stopped. He looked to the west and thought to himself, "The canal, that's where I need to go." Richard turned right and started walking along Montauk Highway.

...

Rachel had just pulled her little Fiat into a parking space behind the Canoe Place Inn. She parked next to a Pontiac LeMans. The bar crowd at the Inn had already arrived and Rachel could hear the music from the live band. She stared at the raindrops on her windshield and tried to decide if she needed an umbrella or not. Her mind drifted back again to the phone call she had received that morning.

The man who called himself Aharon said that he would be wearing a NY Yankee's baseball cap and smoking a cigar. Rachel had decided they should meet under the old green bridge that crossed the Shinnecock Canal. As a teen, she had met many times there with her friends and she knew the place would be deserted, especially on a stormy summer night like this one. The rain was still coming down lightly as she stepped out of her car. As she moved across Newtown Avenue and started heading towards the canal, she heard a deep rumbling in the distance. She regretted her decision regarding the umbrella.

...

Aharon had arrived an hour earlier. He had parked his car behind the big white Inn and headed for the canal. He had just spent the last half hour moving through the numerous side streets and avenues of Hampton Bays to ensure that he wasn't being followed. He had done the same thing earlier in the day before he made his visit to the Levy's red barn on Mill Race Road. He had done two slow drive-bys of the barn while snapping close to fifty photographs with his little Minox camera, the standard issue for anyone in his line of work. On his second drive-by he had seen a little girl walking next to the barn and carrying what looked like an empty bowl, but he could not really tell where she was coming from or where she was going.

Aharon had been doing this kind of a thing for a very long time. He knew it was always best to arrive at a predesignated meeting place at least an hour early and look for signs of a counter-intelligence surveillance operation. If the FBI were onto him and his mission, they would definitely want to cover this meeting. There would be men in surveillance vans or perhaps someone walking a dog. Although the chances were remote that they were present, he would feel much better after he checked the area himself.

Once he had examined the areas under both sides of the bridge and had examined the few boats that the waves were pounding up against the canal's bulkhead, he moved to his meeting spot, put a Yankees baseball cap on his head, and lit up a fine Macanudo cigar.

...

The rain started to fall hard as Rachel approached the underside of the bridge. She could just make out through the rain what appeared to be a man wearing a baseball cap. As she stepped under the cover of the bridge, the man raised his right hand and waved. His right hand held a big cigar. As Rachel approached, he switched the cigar to his left hand and stuck out his right.

He said, "Rachel, I am Aharon. It is so nice to finally meet you."

Rachel gave him her hand but did not say anything. When she finally spoke there was a curt note in her voice. "How did you know my uncle?"

"Ahh," he replied. "Actually, I knew both your father and your uncle. When we were all young men, we fought side-by-side together in a battle that took place in the city of Jerusalem. That was in 1948. Your father left for America shortly after that and your Uncle Yoni and I began our work together in the new Israeli government."

As he talked, they moved closer to the canal's edge. The water was rushing south through the canal like a raging torrent. The lashing rain and wind combined with the deep rumbles of thunder made it difficult for Rachel to hear what Aharon was saying. She leaned in closer as they stood on the edge of the canal's bulkhead.

Aharon continued, "Yoni received many letters from your father over the years that we worked together, and I remember the day he received a letter and a picture telling him all about your birth and what a beautiful baby you were. Yoni would show your picture around and tell anyone who would listen, 'I'm an uncle! I'm an uncle! Look at this beautiful baby girl!'"

He paused for a moment and looked directly into Rachel's eyes and said in a soft voice, "They were both good men."

"And now I want to talk to you about…" he added, but he suddenly stopped talking and his gaze moved from Rachel's eyes to behind her. Rachel quickly turned to see what had caused Aharon to freeze in mid-sentence.

There, standing just six feet away, was a man wearing a light jacket that had been saturated by the rain. The man's hair was plastered to his head and water dripped off him as if he had just had a bucket poured over his head. The man was in a shooting stance, with both hands wrapped around a revolver.

Aharon instinctively moved to step in front of Rachel. He had just begun to move when the man with the gun pulled the trigger. The first bullet hit Aharon squarely in the heart. The force of the bullet's impact lifted him off of his feet and sent his already-dead body spinning into the raging current.

Rachel attempted to grab Aharon before he went over the side, but something forced her body to go in the opposite direction. The second bullet hit her high up on her left shoulder. Before her body could even register the pain, a second bullet tore through her right temple. Her body followed Aaron's path and tumbled over the bulkhead's side and was swept away.

Richard stood staring at the spot where the two strangers had stood conversing just seconds ago. He lowered his gun to his side and walked over to the edge of the canal. At that moment a giant clap of thunder shook the bridge above him. He looked down at his feet and saw the remains of a still-smoldering cigar. He gave it a kick and watched it as it spun in the air and then was swallowed by the black water rushing before him.

In a voice filled with rage and hate he shouted, "Slut, slut, slut!"

Then he turned and headed up the embankment.

Chapter 9

"What Took You So Long?"

Richard spent a long and sleepless night in his hotel room's only chair, gun in hand, with his eyes affixed on the room's doorknob. He was sure the cops would be busting down his door any minute and he wanted to face them as they came rushing in to kill him. He would have fled immediately after the killing, but the rain was so bad he was sure he would just wreck his car, get hurt, and then he would be at their mercy.

The sun had been up for an hour before he finally packed the few things he had in his room and went out to his car.

Now two and a half hours later he found himself driving north on the Hutchinson River Parkway heading for the Tappan Zee Bridge. He looked in his rearview mirror every few minutes. He knew they were there and if he had to drive all the way to Poughkeepsie to lose them he would.

...

The NYPD Detectives from Operation Omega were stationed on the rooftops, in the street and in the lobby of 35 Pine Street in Yonkers, New York. Operation Omega was a special homicide task force established several months earlier by the NYPD and was led by Inspector Timothy Dowd. The task force now consisted of over 300 detectives.

Detective Sergeant John Fallon was one of the six detectives assigned to this surveillance. He was a seasoned homicide detective and had been working on this case for over a year. He sat in a carpet store delivery van that wasn't really a carpet store delivery van about 100 feet from the entrance to 35 Pine Street. He was in radio contact with the two detectives in the lobby, the two detectives on the roof and the one detective at the far end of the block.

Everyone was tired. They had arrived at seven o'clock this morning to relieve the night surveillance shift. Now Fallon's team's twelve-hour shift was just about over. No one really knew what the guy they were looking for looked like, although they had a general description of him. He was a white male, 24 years old, with muscular arms.

It was a car they were watching for. They even had a search warrant to it. It was a yellow 1970 Ford Galaxie and it belonged to the guy who lived in apartment 7E.

. . .

Richard Falco glanced at his watch as he made his turn off of Glenwood Avenue onto Pine Street. The face of his Timex watch told him it was now 6:25 pm. He had been driving for over six hours. The drive and his lack of sleep had made him bleary-eyed. He was looking forward to just crawling into his own bed. He knew he had to talk to his neighbor, but it would have to wait until the morning.

Richard pulled into a parking space just past his building and turned off his car. He didn't even bother to grab his overnight bag. He just opened the car door and stepped into the street. He pushed down the lock, slammed the Ford's door shut, and started walking toward the entrance to number 35 Pine Street.

. . .

The squelch on Detective Sergeant Fallon's hand-held radio broke. He had just been thinking about the chicken parmesan dinner his wife had promised him for this evening. As he was reaching for his radio he heard the detective from the roof's surveillance team call out, "Yellow Ford coming down the block now. It's a Galaxie."

Fallon slid down in his seat and waited for the sound of the car passing his van. As soon as he heard it pass him he lifted his head just high enough to see over his dashboard. He saw the yellow Ford slip into an open parking spot just past the apartment building. The squelch broke again and this time he heard, "He's out…nothing in his hands…he has a jacket on… climbing the steps now."

Fallon said, "Take him by the elevator. I'm coming through the front door right behind him."

Fallon leapt out of the van and sprinted toward the entrance to the building. As he ran up the steps to the entrance he reached into his shirt and pulled out his gold NYPD Detective Sergeant shield that hung around his neck. He yanked the door open with his left hand. With his right, he reached for the Colt Cobra on his hip.

…

Richard Falco entered the lobby of his apartment building and crossed the lobby to the 35 brass mailboxes set into the wall. He reached into his jacket pocket and pulled out his keys. The little mailbox key was the last one on the ring. He stopped in front of the box labeled 7E and inserted his key. He unlocked the box and reached in to pull out his mail. As he was pulling out a small handful of envelopes, he heard the glass front door to the building being opened behind him. Out of the corner of his left eye he could see two shapes moving towards him from the elevator.

As he turned towards the shapes, he dropped the mail from his hand and reached for his waistband. Suddenly he felt a piece of cold steel pressed tightly up against the back of his head and he heard the metallic click of a hammer being pulled back.

He heard a voice say, "Move, motherfucker, and I will blow your head off." That is when his bladder let go.

He felt several pairs of hands pressing his face and body into the mailboxes. He felt his gun being ripped from its waist band, and then he felt handcuffs being snapped tightly around his wrists.

…

Detective Sergeant Fallon spun around the handcuffed man and looked him straight in the eyes. He knew he was looking at a true monster. The handcuffed man smiled at him and asked, "What took you so long?"

Detective Fallon turned to the other two detectives and said, "Put him in my car."

With that, the man who recently found out that he was adopted, and who now called himself by his birth name Richard Falco, was hustled to a waiting police car.

Fallon reached to the small of his back and removed the revolver he had just taken from the suspect. He noted that it was a .44-caliber Charter Arms Bulldog. He then reached down to the floor to pick up the mail the suspect had dropped.

He turned over one of the envelopes and saw that it was the Consolidated Edison electric bill for the resident of Apartment 7E. The name on the front of the envelope was David Berkowitz.

As Detective Fallon reached the street, one of the detectives from his team approached and said, "Come over here and look at what we found."

Fallon walked over to the open trunk of David Berkowitz's 1970 yellow Ford Galaxie and peered inside. There, lying in the trunk on top of some brown paper wrapping, was a .45 caliber machine gun.

...

Captain Keenan was the Duty Officer inside the communications room at One Police Plaza in downtown Manhattan that evening. It was now 6:50 pm and he was staring down at a handwritten note just handed to him by one of the dispatchers. He folded the note in half and ran for the stairs. Less than one minute later he was standing in front of a large wooden door. The name plaque on the door read, "Michael J. Codd, Commissioner."

Keenan knocked on the door and heard a voice say, "Come in."

Keenan stepped into the room and saw Commissioner Codd reading a report at this desk. The Commissioner did not look up.

Captain Keenan stepped to the front of the desk and said, "Commissioner, I have a communication that you should see, right now sir."

With that the Commissioner looked up and took the slip of paper from Keenan's hand. He unfolded it, looked down and saw the words, "Son of Sam in custody."

...

Rachel Levy was reported missing by a friend three days after the arrest of the Son of Sam. No connection was ever made between her disappearance and the multiple killings in New York City of young women by this infamous serial killer.

Seven days after the arrest of David Berkowitz, who was also known as Richard Falco and the Son of Sam, the local police in Southampton located Rachel's car behind the Canoe Place Inn. An examination of the vehicle found no evidence of violence. No additional fingerprints were found in or on the vehicle. A second abandoned car was also found behind the Canoe Place Inn. It was a late model Pontiac LeMans that had been rented from the Avis Rental Car counter at Newark Airport and was now overdue. The individual who had rented the car was a Mr. Aharon Kagan with an address of 16 Worthington Road, Paramus, New Jersey. Police inquiries made regarding this individual indicated no previous criminal record. Further inquiries indicated that the address of 16 Worthington Road, Paramus, New Jersey did not exist.

Chapter 10

The Death Toll Grows

A great many bad things had happened to Betsy Vail in the past week. Her mother had said that she was suffering from a bad case of the flu. Five days ago, while her mother was at the Rexall in town, Betsy had snuck out of her house and visited the barn one last time. She had dropped to her knees to look under that rusty old Bell Telephone truck. There lay Sir Lancelot and her kittens, all dead.

As the days passed, Betsy became weaker. She could no longer eat or hold down fluids. Her mother took her to see Doctor Saffer at the Medical Center on Ponquogue Avenue twice. On the second visit, her mother had to carry her into the building.

This time Doctor Saffer called an ambulance and she was taken to Southampton hospital. It took several days of tests before a diagnosis could be made. Betsy's mother and father took turns sitting next to her bed in the intensive care unit the whole time.

A young resident by the name of Dr. Hammond had been treating Betsy from the moment she entered the emergency room. He now sat with both parents just outside of Betsy's room. He told them that the test results indicated that Betsy was suffering from acute radiation sickness, also sometimes called ARS. He said that some people do recover from this, but recovery is more difficult with children and the elderly. He questioned them as to how Betsy might have been exposed, but they had no idea how it could have happened.

Ten days later, Betsy's heart failed. The deaths attributed to that rusty old Bell Telephone truck and its cargo, tucked away in a little red barn in Hampton Bays, now totaled five.

There were many more to come.

PART 3

January 2018

Chapter 11

Another Day at the Office

Jake Tucker pounded his feet on the floor of the surveillance van and said, “I have never been this freakin’ cold in my entire life!"

The moment he stopped talking, his teeth began to chatter again. The man sitting next to him was also shivering. He was NYPD Detective George Lazanski. He was glaring at Jake and finally he said, “You know, I never liked you.”

As they bantered back and forth, their eyes never left the video screen hanging on the interior wall of the van.

Suffolk County Police Homicide Detective Jake Tucker had been a cop for 20 years, ever since he entered the Suffolk County Police Department as a 22-year-old straight out of college. For the last 6 years he had been assigned to the homicide squad. Like many people in his line of work he considered what he did for a living as more of a “calling” then an actual job.

Having grown up in a very small town on the eastern end of Long Island, he had always believed that there was a good chance he would end up working in the summer tourist industry which was so prevalent among the small towns that dotted the landscape along the Island’s south fork. Jake had no illusions as to who he was or what his limitations were. He strongly believed that it was not his job to solve the problems of the world. He knew he couldn’t, even if he wanted to. But to him, it always came down to those innocents who were made to suffer at the hands of others. There was so much suffering in the world and so much of it could be prevented simply by removing the truly evil from society. Jake believed that he could reduce some of that suffering by simply tracking down and arresting killers and thereby preventing them from killing again.

Jake's personal life was stereotypical for a police detective in this day and age. He had divorced a decade ago; had no children; had few friends and was a first-class former drunk. Although he never crossed over that fine line into true alcoholism, he had come very, very close.

Jake had an on-again, off-again relationship with a divorced art teacher by the name of Kirstin from the local high school. She was in her mid-thirties, real cute and full of energy. They had started dating about two years ago and then one day she decided that she wanted to get back together with her ex-husband Billy who had promised to seek professional help and be a better person, blah, blah, blah.

Billy was Billy Burke. He, like Jake, was a lifelong resident of Hampton Bays. It is pretty much a guarantee that if you are divorced and live in small town like Hampton Bays, sooner or later you are going to run into your ex. That's what happened to Jake and Kirstin on their second date. It happened just inside the Villa Paul restaurant in town. They were waiting to be seated when Kirstin's ex-husband approached them. Although there was no major scene, Jake's instincts, as well as all the little hairs on the back of his neck, told him there was something seriously wrong with Billy Burke.

Jake did a little checking with some detective colleagues from the local police department and found out that Billy was a methhead. Jake, having never worked narcotics cases, did a little research into methamphetamine addiction just so that he would have a clear understanding of what he might have to deal with someday. He still remembers reading the line that said, "...it is usually a hopeless condition that causes irreparable brain and central nervous system damage."

What concerned Jake the most was the passage that read, "...usually devoted to solely getting the drug of their choice and will commit crimes against loved ones as easily as against strangers." He knew then that Billy Burke had the potential for physically hurting people.

Jake had been surprised and a little hurt when Kirstin told him that she was going to give her marriage another try. However, in the end they separated on good terms and had made a point of checking in with each other once in a while via email. A couple of months after the breakup Jake ran into her one early morning at the Starbucks in town. It was a hot summer morning and she was wearing a long-sleeve turtle neck sweater. She had a deep purple bruise on her right cheek that she had tried, quite unsuccessfully, to cover with makeup. Jake knew what he was looking at and she knew that he knew. At the end of the conversation she said she would call if she needed help. Jake told her she needed help now. She shook her head no and left the Starbucks with tears in her eyes.

After their chance meeting at Starbucks, Jake decided to pay a little visit to Billy Burke. It wasn't out of love. His and Kirstin's relationship had never gotten that far. It was that suffering thing.

Jake chose a Wednesday evening. He remembered that Kirstin was a longtime member of the St. Rosalie's Choir and that they practiced every Wednesday evening at the church. It didn't take a lot of hard thinking to know where Billy was going to be. He certainly wouldn't be sitting home when there were drugs to score, and drugs were normally scored in a little park just seven miles away along the Peconic River in the town of Riverhead. So, Jake did his thing and followed Billy into the park on a quiet Wednesday evening. He watched him make his score. Billy then found a secluded bench and did the only thing that Billy Burke was capable of doing and that was getting high.

Jake approached the bench from the rear and wrapped his left arm around Billy's chin and yanked Billy's head upward. Billy's throat was fully exposed and his hands were pawing at Jake's arm. His legs began kick and flail like a man who was being hung. Billy stopped his thrashing the moment he saw the glistening eight-inch silver blade being held in front of him. The tip of the blade was now pressing into the soft spot directly under his chin. That is when good ole' Billy Burke began to cry. Jake slowly lowered his lips to the side of Billy's head and whispered, "Hit Kirstin again and next time I will take a trophy. Now, blink your eyes if you understand."

Jake wasn't absolutely sure of what, if any, effect he had on curbing Billy Burke's violent tendencies towards Kirsten. He did know that the list of things that he would need to fully explain on judgement day had just gotten a little longer. He hadn't seen or heard from Kirsten in several months. But he had read in the local paper that a longtime resident of Hampton Bays by the name of Billy Burke had recently died of a drug overdose in a small park along the Peconic River in the town of Riverhead.

Today was a typical day at the office for Jake Tucker. He and his NYPD friend were sitting down the block from a brownstone building on West 48th Street in Manhattan that they had been watching for 9 hours. There was another van like theirs parked at the other end of the block. The Arctic temperature inside the van was due to an outside temperature of 9 degrees and a 30-mile-per-hour wind coming right of the Hudson River and barreling right up 48th Street. Add that to the fact that they could not run the engine without blowing their surveillance, and both men now felt as if they were slabs of beef hanging from hooks in a meat locker.

Jake Tucker had been hunting for murder suspect Sean Connelly for 2 months. He had finally found a witness to the stabbing death of a local drug dealer that had taken place on Fire Island that past summer. The homicide took place at a gay beach called Cherry Grove and it happened during one of the many "Tea Times." Unbeknownst to Jake at the time there were many different types of Tea Time. There was Tea, Low Tea, High Tea, Middle Tea, Junior Tea, Senior Tea, and a few more with descriptive names that were interesting to say the least. Of course, there is never any actual tea. It is simply the local code for "Let's start drinking!" and it usually begins around four o'clock in the afternoon and ends around four o'clock in the morning.

On this one particular early summer morning last August, a Mr. Sean Connelly had a disagreement with a Mr. James Spats. According to a witness, Mr. Connelly had made a purchase the day before of some mind-altering party favors from the resident dealer Mr. James Spats. Turns out the party favors were nothing but pancake batter mixed with baking soda. When Sean was out walking with his paramour Walter early the next morning, he spotted Mr. Spats on the boardwalk. Sean began the conversation by grabbing Mr. Spats by his throat and demanding his money back.

Things went downhill rather quickly from there. According to Sean's now-jilted lover Walter, Sean ended the conversation by plunging the blade of his big Buck knife six or eight times into Mr. Spats' chest. Walter said he wasn't absolutely sure how many times Mr. Spats was stabbed because he lost count.

Jake, with arrest warrant in hand, had been looking for Sean ever since the day that Walter signed a sworn statement.

The ever revengeful and jilted lover Walter had telephoned Jake yesterday to let him know that Sean, who had gone dark, was now staying with his Aunt Kate on West 48th Street in Manhattan.

It turned out that Sean Connelly was well known to the NYPD. He was a suspect in at least two other homicides and had multiple arrests for assaults and robberies.

It seemed that Sean Connelly was part of a dying breed of gangsters, who considered himself one of the last remaining "Westies." The Westies of the past were a New York City-based Irish American organized crime gang, responsible for racketeering, drug trafficking, and contract killing all throughout the city. They mostly operated out of the neighborhood known as Hell's Kitchen in Manhattan, generally considered the area west of Eighth Avenue, between 34th and 59th Streets. The Westies were not a large organization. According to NYPD Intelligence they never seemed to have more than two dozen members, even in their heyday. Now, the old neighborhood families had been replaced by a diverse population of young people involved with the theater and, more recently, by Wall Street financiers.

According to the NYPD file, Sean's last arrest didn't go very well. It seemed that members of an ATF/NYPD Task Force had an arrest warrant for Sean. On one bright early morning last fall Sean was just leaving his Aunt Kate's brownstone when he spotted the arresting officers coming down the block. He bolted and headed west on 48th Street. The foot chase ended up going all the way to the wharf along the Hudson River. At some point Sean had decided that his best chance of escape was to jump into the Hudson. Unfortunately for Sean, the Belgian Malinois that had just been let loose by an ATF Agent made the same decision. Sean found it very difficult to swim away from the police with a really pissed-off 75-pound Malinois attached to his leg. However, in the end, none of it mattered.

The only eyewitness in that particular homicide case failed to identify Sean in a court-ordered lineup. It seemed that Sean refused to participate in the lineup, so Sean turned out to be the only one of the eighty guys in the lineup to be physically dragged to the viewing glass, at which time he proceeded to raise his legs off the ground and kick out the one-way viewing glass. The witness trying to make the identification was covered in shards of glass. As Sean was kicking away, he was also spitting directly into the faces of the three DA investigators trying to hold on to him. Two things happened that day. First, the only eyewitness to the murder was unable to identify Sean as the suspect. Second, all of the DA Investigators had to be screened for syphilis. It turned out Sean was a carrier.

Detective Jake Tucker and Detective George Lazanski had known each other for a long time. They had met one early morning on the side of the Long Island Expressway about 10 years ago. Jake was driving a precinct sector car then and had chased a pickup truck onto the Expressway. Once the pickup truck had pulled over, Jake checked on the radio to see if the truck was stolen. He then got out of his patrol car and as he approached the truck two guys and a girl jumped out and proceeded to beat the crap out of him. He had managed to knock one of guys out cold with a little something special he kept in his back pocket for just these types of situations. However, the other two had him on his back and he was losing this round badly. All of a sudden the male that was sitting on his chest just disappeared. Jake threw the female off of him and then cuffed her. That's when he looked around and saw this guy putting cuffs onto the guy who had been pounding on him just a minute ago.

The guy with the cuffs turned out to be NYPD patrolman George Lazanski, who had finished his 4-12 shift a couple of hours ago and was now on his way home to Lake Ronkonkoma. Six court appearances and one criminal trial later they became good friends.

"Did I mention I never liked you?" asked a shivering Lazanski for the third time.

Jake replied, "Hey, how come these things never go like on TV? You know, the cops pull up on a bright sunny day all dressed in Hawaiian shirts. They start watching whatever they're watching, and the bad guy shows up before the next Viagra commercial."

Lazanski said, "Yeah, and no matter how much coffee they drink they never have to - - There he is!"

On the monitor Jake saw Sean Connelly, with his flaming red hair, coming down the steps of his aunt's building.

The surveillance team at the other end of the block had already stepped out of their van and split up, with each taking a different side of the street. Jake and George did the same thing. Connelly was a runner and it was important that he be boxed in order to avoid a repeat of what happened last fall. Besides, they didn't have a dog with them today. Jake was on the same side of the street as Connelly and was rapidly closing the distance.

Fortunately for Jake, the biting wind was hitting Connelly right in the face which caused Connelly to look downward. Jake made sure not to make eye contact. He wanted to appear to be just some stranger passing him in the street. He even moved to the far righthand side of the sidewalk as they got closer. That kind of body language signals the other guy that you're making room for him as you pass each other. The trick to this situation is to change direction and slam into the bad guy in between blinks.

This is precisely what Jake did. As Jake slammed into Connelly, he grabbed Connelly's shoulders and forced him chest-first into the wrought iron fence that separated the sidewalk from the apartment building's first floor windows.

Unfortunately, this is when all the trouble started.

Sean Connelly hadn't put on a hat for the same reason he didn't button up his coat. He wasn't planning on being outside very long. In fact, he was only going two buildings down from his aunt's house to visit a friend. The fact that his thick coat was unbuttoned contributed to his somewhat accidental impaling. The wrought iron fencing that Mr. Connelly was thrown onto was of the type that had the sharp pointy finials sticking straight up. This was a very common architectural feature with New York City brownstone apartment buildings. Add this to the fact that Jake threw his entire weight onto the back of the bent-over Connelly, and you end up with a really deep puncture wound.

Hello ambulance.

Hello Internal Affairs.

Chapter 12

Moving in Day

Jack Ford had just unloaded the last of his and his mother' boxes from the back of his Dodge pickup truck.

He stood on his newly rented property on Mill Race Road in Hampton Bays and slowly turned in a circle. Spring was just around the corner and he expected there would be a great deal of foliage on the property. He especially liked the seclusion and the closeness to the creek that was just a few hundred feet from the property.

Ford also liked the old broken-down barn. He knew he would have to get around to going in there one of these days. He had some ideas for that place.

The real estate agent told him that the house had been purchased by a local real estate investor for nonpayment of taxes a number of years ago and that maintenance on the house had been done twice a year for several decades. Over those years, the real estate investor had allowed many of his extended family members to live in the home for short periods of time. Six months ago, the investor had passed away and the property was promptly made available as a rental by one of its inheritors.

Jack Ford had been looking for a place like this to live for some time. All he needed was room for himself and his aged mother, Celia. Celia Ford was 85 years old and still got around pretty well. As long as there were not a lot of stairs to climb, she could still move around the house and take care of herself.

Jack Ford had spent his early years as an Explosives Ordnance Disposal technician with the U.S. Army. He had received his basic explosives handling training right after boot camp at Fort Dix in New Jersey. He then spent close to three years assigned to various military bases around the world. After his 4-year commitment with the military was completed, he spent a number of years working at Grumman Aerospace in Calverton.

He was now a machinist by trade and would make parts to specifications using various machine tools like lathes and milling machines. He liked to tell people that he worked on the later production model of the F-14 Tomcat, although in fact he had simply milled a replacement pin for a new type of landing gear that was being tested. After Grumman had been bought out by Northrop and relocated to Maryland, Ford had gotten a job as a machinist at an industrial roll-up door manufacturer in Bellport. His hobbies included collecting guns and explosives. He had quite a collection of the latter. In fact, on his last day of employment at Grumman he had helped himself to 2 cases of explosive bolts used to separate the F-14 Tomcat canopy from the fuselage right before the pilot ejected.

The guns, explosives and extra food stores he kept in his basement were all part of his survival plans. He fully expected there to be a major revolt against the government at any time and he wanted to be prepared. He also wanted to participate in that revolt when that great day came around.

As far as Ford was concerned, every politician in the country regardless of their political party had been put on this earth for one purpose and one purpose alone. It was to make his life miserable. As a reminder as to what was coming, he kept a large plaque hanging on the wall above his bed. That plaque had hung above his bed in every house he had lived in since he was 22 years old. The plaque was a quotation from one of Ford's favorite writers and simply said, "*There are only nine meals between mankind and total anarchy.*"

He had a lot more than nine meals put away and he was definitely looking forward to the anarchy.

Ford had been living in the house with his mother for about a month when one of his old acquaintances showed up at the door with a suitcase in his hand. The guy's name was Zabo Pruit. Ford and Pruit had both worked at Grumman for a number of years. Pruit worked in the maintenance department and it was clear that he always would. Like Ford, Zabo Pruit was a thief and had helped himself to a great deal of his employer's property over the years. As a matter of fact, Zabo made it a point to steal at least one thing every single day that he worked at the Grumman Calverton facility.

On most days it was just a simple hand tool like a wrench or a hammer. Zabo had stolen so many tools that his house looked like a Sears Tool Store after an earthquake. Zabo had covered every flat surface in his home with a hand tool. This included tables, chairs, cabinets and floor spaces throughout his entire house and garage.

Zabo had a fetish for any kind of tool. Some he liked to keep. Some he liked to sell. His tastes ran from the smallest hand shovel to full size construction cranes. He and one of his fences once actually stole a 5-ton crane right off a road construction site on the Long Island Expressway. No one was caught and the theft was never traced to him, although local law enforcement had their suspicions.

It was his love for tools that made him apply for a job at the Home Depot out on Sunrise Highway. Unfortunately, he got caught late one evening trying to load an industrial air compressor into the back of an accomplice's pickup truck. He was fired the next morning and the store filed felony criminal charges. After his arrest, Zabo decided he no longer wanted to deal with the criminal justice system. So he stopped answering the calls from his court-appointed lawyer and refused to show up to court on his various hearing dates.

It was this decision that caused him to be on the front porch of his friend Jack Ford's home in Hampton Bays.

Jack Ford stood on his front porch staring down at Zabo. His gaze moved to the suitcase in Zabo's hand and he finally asked, "What's with the suitcase?"

Zabo replied, "My wife called me and said the cops were at my house. They said they have a warrant for me so I can't go home for a while. I was hoping you could put me up for a few days."

"You know I have my mother here. She's getting senile and will absolutely freak out if she sees a stranger in the house. Isn't there anyplace else you can go?"

"Not really," said Zabo. "Come on, man, I can stay in your basement. It's just a couple of days."

Ford lied and said, "I don't have a basement. But I do have an old barn on the other side of the property. You can crash there for a few days. Park your car behind the barn so that it can't be seen from the road. I'll bring you out a kerosene lantern and sleeping bag. Don't burn the place down. Give me five minutes and I'll meet you back there."

Five minutes later Ford was standing with Zabo at the side door to the barn. Ford, to his dismay, had not been given any keys to the padlocks for the barn's doors. But he did have a crowbar. He hooked the crowbar behind the hasp and pushed up. The hasp, along with the lock, fell to the ground in an instant.

Zabo, suitcase in hand, pulled open the door and stepped inside. Multiple holes in the roof provided light in the barn. There were a few long handled tools lying across the doorway. Both men stepped over these and walked up to what looked like an old Bell Telephone Company van. You could barely make out the letters and logo on the side panel.

Zabo said, "Man, I haven't seen one of these in years."

"Me neither," replied Ford.

The van was heavily rusted over and all four tires were flat. The van was parked directly under the largest hole in the roof and it was clear that the van had been exposed to snow and rain for quite a few years.

Zabo and Ford circled the van trying all of the doors. All of the doors appeared to be locked.

Zabo turned to Ford and said, "I wonder if there's anything valuable in there?"

Ford, ever mindful of Zabo's thieving ways, said, "I'll open it another time." He pointed to a far corner of the barn and said, “That’s probably the driest spot over there. I’ll bring some food out to you after dinner.”

Zabo was staring at the spot Ford had just pointed out. There was a clear look of skepticism on his face. When Ford saw this he said, “Hey, beggars and people being hunted by the cops can’t be choosy. You feel free to stay someplace else if you want. I promise you, my feelings won’t be hurt.” With that, Ford left the barn and headed for the house.

Chapter 13

Germaphobia is Alive and Well

The incident involving Sean Connelly ended up not being such a big deal. Jake attributed this good fortune to the fact that the arrest took place on the west side of Manhattan and not on the squeaky clean streets of Suffolk County. Connelly's court appointed attorney tried to bring up the issue of police brutality several times during press interviews but the local press just didn't seem interested in portraying a New York City street thug, who committed a homicide in a Long Island gay community, as a victim.

Jake was now sitting at his desk in the Homicide Squad room finishing the last of his reports on the Connelly case. He had a clear view of the Lieutenant's office from where he sat and could see the new squad Lieutenant and his Admin officer having a conversation in the office. Jake pushed back in his chair and shook his head in frustration. Just as Jake started to believe he had dodged a bullet over the Connelly arrest, another problem popped up right in front of him.

This one had to do with his new Homicide Squad Lieutenant. Lieutenant Bob Blair was straight out of the 1960s. He had a reputation for being the dimmest bulb in the room, no matter what room he was in or how many people were in that room. He had a disdain for any type of modern forensic techniques including face recognition software and "familial DNA." One of his favorite lines was, "If you do your job right, you don't need any of that fancy computer crap." Of course, in his mind "Doing your job right" meant handcuffing a guy to a table and interrogating him for 10 straight hours. The fact that Lieutenant Blair's brother was the President of the police union caused lots of tongues to wag when his transfer was first announced.

However, none of this was really a problem for Jake. He had spent a lot of time in his career working his way around bad police bosses. The problem was Lieutenant Blair's admin guy, who wasn't actually a guy. Her name was Detective Jillian Stark. She and Jake had worked in the 3rd Precinct together as patrolmen for about 3 years. They both decided on the very first day they met that they did not like each other.

On the day they first met she was relieving him at the end of his shift. She had only been out of the academy for a short time, but for some reason there was no training officer with her. Jake had just gassed the sector car and handed her the keys. Unfortunately for Jake, he had left one of those little red plastic stirring sticks you get with your Starbucks coffee on the floor of the car.

She was just about to climb in when she stopped, pointed at the stirrer and shouted, "What the hell is that? How am I supposed to drive this car now? You're supposed to make sure the car is clean before you hand it over to the next person!"

Jake stared at her for a moment. He wasn't quite sure she was serious. He then decided he didn't want to know if she was serious or not. He bent down and picked up the stirrer. Without saying a word he walked away and entered the Precinct. Twenty minutes later he was climbing into his personal car behind the precinct when he looked up and saw that his sector car was still parked where he had left it. Suddenly he saw Patrolman Stark back out of the passenger side of the vehicle. She had a cloth rag in one hand and a spray can of Lysol in the other. She was also wearing surgical gloves and a surgical mask. He noticed that all the floor mats had been pulled out of the car. She dropped to her knees and began spraying Lysol on each of the mats and then wiping them down. All during this process he could actually hear her talking to herself from across the parking lot.

Jake thought back to the Minnesota Multiphasic Personality Exam he had to go through when he was an applicant for patrolman. He thought to himself, "I thought that test was supposed to weed out people like this."

As he started his car, he looked up at her one more time. It appeared that her can of Lysol had run out and she just kicked the empty can across the parking lot. What really bothered him the most about this situation was that she was supposed to be on patrol. He decided at that point that this was a person that he would make an effort to stay away from.

Now that Detective Stark was the new Admin person for the homicide squad, Jake suspected trouble. To make matters worse, she was sleeping with the Lieutenant. It wasn't the fact that they were both married to other people that bothered him. As far as Jake was concerned, who they spent their personal time with was none of his business. What worried him was the position that she held. Although technically she did not outrank anyone in the squad, her position as Admin officer put her in a position to do some real damage.

There had already been one incident and Jack expected there to be a lot more.

It had to do with one of Holly Gilpin's cases. Holly was Jamaican and she was the closest thing to a friend that Jake had in the homicide squad. She was an 8-year veteran of the squad and probably one of the best, if not the best, Detectives in the department. She was the person that all the other Detectives, male and female, went to when they ran out of ideas on how to proceed with a difficult homicide investigation.

Jake had heard that Holly was about to arrest an MS-13 gang member for a particularly gruesome murder. All the bosses had been briefed and the DA's Homicide Bureau had signed off on the arrest. Just a few hours before the arrest was to occur Holly was approached by Detective Stark who wanted to be briefed on the investigation. The ever-polite Holly simply said that she had already briefed Lieutenant Blair and that she would be happy to fill in Stark at a later time. However, at that moment she was busy planning the final details with Emergency Services for the arrest of a potentially violent suspect. Detective Stark stood over Holly's desk and stared down at her in silence for a full 30 seconds. She then turned on her heels and walked away. Six minutes later, Holly's desk phone rang. It was Lieutenant Blair. He simply said, "Hold off on the arrest in the MS-13 case. I think we need to review the investigation again."

Jake always expected to be second guessed. It was part of the job and usually came from the press, the brass or the DA's office. That wasn't the issue. What bothered him, and the rest of the homicide squad, was being second-guessed by an inexperienced Detective whose only claim to fame was that she was having sex with the boss.

Jake went back to working on the files on his desk.

When he looked up again, the formerly busy squad room was just about empty. He saw that a few of the night shift detectives had just walked into the room. He glanced over to the Lieutenant's office and saw that the lights were off. Jake got up from his desk, gave the obligatory nod hello to a few of the night shift detectives, and headed for the door.

He had promised earlier in the day to stop at the local cop bar on the way home. The place was called "The Maples" and was only a couple of miles from police headquarters. The unique thing about The Maples was that it was also a biker bar and yet all parties seemed to get along just fine. One of the guys who had been with the Homicide Squad for 5 years had taken a transfer to the DA's office and Jake promised to attend the little impromptu going away party. Jake didn't drink anymore, but would be happy to stand around with a club soda in his hand and swap overly embellished stories with the group.

As he pulled into the dirt parking lot, he spotted his new Lieutenant and his Admin officer getting out of her little red Porsche Boxster. Jake circled the parking lot, pulled back onto the main road and headed for his home in Hampton Bays.

Chapter 14

Two Bad Guys and a Plan

Zabo had spent a restless night in the barn. Ford's suggestion to set up his sleeping bag and lantern in the corner was a good one. Being over twenty feet away from the Bell Telephone Company van would probably prolong his life by a couple of days, or at least it would have if his larceny-driven curiosity had not gotten the better of him. As he lay there trying to fall asleep he was struck by the utter stillness that surrounded him. He had always thought that barns would hold all types of wildlife like mice, pigeons and bats. Especially a barn with lots of holes in the roof like this one. However, he heard nothing but the sound of his own heart beating away in his chest. That was the only sound he heard before he fell asleep.

When Zabo awoke he decided that he would drive to the local Starbucks on Montauk Highway. He liked their egg sandwiches. As he was about to leave the barn he spotted the crowbar that Ford had used the day before to pry the padlock off the door of the barn. He reached down and picked it up and then glanced over at the rusted van. It occurred to him that if there was something valuable inside, Ford probably wouldn't share it with him. He looked back to the crowbar and then again to the van. He looked like a man struggling with a difficult math problem.

Finally, he decided what to do. He would concoct a story that there were rats in the barn and he needed to get off the barn's floor and that is why he pried open the van's back door. He decided he would throw his sleeping bag inside just to make it look good. With that thought, Zabo stepped to the back of the van and got to work with the crowbar.

As Zabo was working up a sweat in the barn, Jack Ford sat 200 yards away at this kitchen table with a copy of the daily newspaper in his hands. He sipped his coffee and murmured continuously to himself about the various ignorant fools that were running the government. It wasn't just those crazy bastards in Washington; Ford was convinced that the parade of fools marched right down the main street in Hampton Bays on a daily basis. He dropped his newspaper down onto the remains of his eggs, stood up and thought to himself, "Somebody's gotta do something about this."

It was the same phrase that he had been repeating to himself every morning for the last 20 years.

Zabo stood at the back of the van and looked through the now open doors. The light inside the van was very dim. He squinted to try and make out the shapes of the items on the floor of the van. There appeared to be eight containers of some kind and a couple of wooden pallets. Zabo finally decided that he needed to get a closer look and stepped up into the van. Before he had even taken one step forward Zabo Pruit received enough radiation to kill a dozen men.

As he moved forward, he stepped on something crunchy. He looked down and saw what looked like the now-crushed bones of a small animal. He thought to himself, "See, I was right, rats."

As he got closer he saw that one of the containers had fallen over. Its thick lid was lying about a foot away and there were some pieces of grey colored metal on the floor of the van that had spilled out of the container.

His first thought was, "Precious metals?"

His second thought was, "Shit, Ford's going to think I went snooping and knocked this thing over."

With that worry in mind, Zabo bent down and attempted to upright the container. In doing so, he realized that all of the containers were made of concrete. In his second attempt, he planted both of his feet against the wall of the van and pushed as hard as he could. Once the cast was righted, he reached down to the floor and collected the grey pieces of metal. He dropped them into the concrete cast and attempted to lift the lid. After lots of grunting and groaning he finally managed to lift it into place.

Unbeknownst to Zabo, he had just done what it took 10 men at NUMEC to do 53 years ago. Those men, working one at a time and being timed with a stop watch, stood behind thick lead shielding and had used a system of remote pulleys and cables to load the 25 pounds Cobalt-60 into this one lead-lined concrete cast. It had taken them eight hours.

Zabo was drenched in sweat. He looked around the inside of the van one more time while thinking how much he regretted his decision to open the van's door. As he was about to leave the van, his eyes settled on a very faded symbol that had been painted long ago onto the side of the concrete cast. He quickly looked at the other casts and saw that they too had the same symbol.

He thought to himself, "What the hell is that?"

He reached into his pocket for his cell phone and stepped back towards the rear doors of the van. He wanted to get a picture of all eight of the casts. He hit the camera icon and took a quick shot. Then he got down on his knees and leaned forward to get a close look at the markings. He saw that the symbol was a faded yellow and black color. He sat back on his haunches and said, "Oh, shit."

Zabo left the barn and headed straight to Ford's front porch. As he approached the door, Ford was just coming out. He had two cups of coffee in his hands.

Ford said, "Thought you might like some coffee. How was the barn?"

Zabo said, "You got rats. They were all around me last night. Look, I hope you don't get mad, but I slept in the van last night, because of all the rats. I popped the lock on the back so I could get in."

Ford looked directly into Zabo's eyes and said, "No problem. Anything in there?"

"Yeah," said Zabo. "Something real interesting." Zabo then proceeded to tell Ford about the eight concrete casts and the symbols painted on their sides.

"You're kidding me," Ford said.

"Nope," replied Zabo. "Come and see for yourself."

An hour later, both men were sitting in Starbucks and talking about what had been discovered in the barn. They had picked a table next to the window that looked out directly onto Montauk Highway. Both had ordered coffee and Zabo had ordered his favorite egg white sandwich. The sandwich lay untouched in front of him. While they were in the barn, Ford had had the great idea of looking at the date of the van's faded inspection sticker to try and figure out how long it might have been in the barn. The sticker indicated that it had last been inspected in January 1965. Zabo offered that the concrete casts may have been stolen and hidden in the barn years ago.

Finally, Ford asked, "Think they're worth anything?"

"I don't know," said Zabo. "But first we'll have to find out if there's still radioactive stuff inside."

"If we do that, what then?" asked Ford.

"Then I call my friend Patti and see what he can do for us." Patti was Patti Ball. He was a wanna-be organized crime guy who liked to hang out with the various made guys in New York City at places like the Ravenite Social Club on Mulberry Street. Every once in a while, one of the family bosses would let Patti be his driver for the day. This was a great honor and added a great deal to Patti's credibility when it came to his true line of work as a professional fence.

Patti had been moving stolen goods for years and he was really good at it. It didn't matter what it was, he could find a buyer. There was the usual jewelry, cars, trucks, heavy equipment and computers. There was also the unusual like a Bengal Tiger or a 2-person submarine. Patti had one price for everything and everybody. He paid you ten cents on the dollar. No more, no less. When he got paid, you got paid, and he never stiffed anybody. This is probably why he had managed to live so long.

Patti also had a quasi-legitimate business that he ran in nearby Manorville. It was an asbestos transportation company. Basically, once some big company was done pulling all of the asbestos out of a building and putting it into sealed bags, the bags would then have to be shipped to a proper disposal facility. That was Patti's company's job. With all the business that there was in New York City, Patti kept his trucks on the road around the clock. Another key benefit for Patti and his stolen goods business was that no one ever wanted to open up the asbestos bags to see what was really inside.

Zabo had left the table to go to the men's room. Ford had begun to consider other possibilities than just selling this stuff. It was important not to rush into anything. There was a good chance that the Bell Telephone Company van had been in that barn for fifty years and it didn't look like it would be going anywhere soon. His biggest problem was Zabo. He had a mouth on him and would probably tell ten different people about this by the end of the day. Just as that worrisome thought ended, Zabo returned to the table.

Ford looked up at him and said, "You don't look so good, man."

"Yeah," said Zabo. "I think I'm coming down with something. I just lost my coffee."

"Well, stay away from me and the house. If my mother gets the flu, it's all over for her." Zabo simply nodded his head as they stood up to leave.

By the time Zabo arrived back at the barn it was midday and he was feeling awful. He did manage to call his wife from his cell phone while Ford was inside a convenience store buying some milk. He told her he was staying with his friend Ford and asked her to get Patti Ball's number from his old address book on top of the refrigerator. Ball's number was one of those that he would never put into his cell phone. Zabo quickly ended the call with his wife and dialed Patti Ball's number. While he was doing this, he kept one watchful eye on the door to the convenience store.

When Ford returned to the pickup truck he told Zabo, "Again, we have to keep this thing quiet until we know what we have. Don't blab to anyone. I think I know where to get a Geiger counter but it will take a few days, maybe a week.

In the meantime, I'll start reading up on this stuff as soon as I get home from work tomorrow night." He added, "There's a library in town. We passed it on the way here. Since you're not working why don't you go there tomorrow and read up on this radiation stuff? You said there was writing on the casts. Why don't you take a picture of the writing with your cell phone and then try and look the stuff up?" He continued, "Besides, it will give you something to do while you are hiding from the cops."

That conversation outside the convenience store was less than an hour ago, but to Zabo it felt like days. He didn't understand how he could feel so bad, so fast. His mind went briefly to the symbols on the concrete casts but he dismissed the idea. It had to be the flu.

It was getting harder to concentrate and there appeared to be gaps in his memory. All of a sudden he felt confused about everything. He kept telling himself over and over again that he must have a really bad bug banging around inside of him. He was now running a fever and retching every few minutes. He also had a searing pain in his intestines. He felt as if they were being tied into knots.

He decided he needed to get some help. He remembered seeing a sign for a medical building when he came into town. Maybe it was one of those walk-in clinics. He did seem to remember it was somewhere near that diner you pass when you come into town. Zabo got up from the floor of the barn and staggered to his car. His vision was blurry and both of his hands were trembling. He had difficulty putting the key into the ignition and starting the car.

He finally got control of himself and put his car into gear. He started down Mill Race Road and turned right onto Springville. He was fading in and out now and it took all of his strength just to keep his car on the road. He could no longer remember which road he had to take to get to Montauk Highway. He passed roads named "Wakeman" and "Foster." He passed another road on his left, but he could no longer read the green and white street sign.

All of a sudden everything went black. He awoke for a brief moment and realized that his car was sitting in water. He looked out the windshield and saw his car was now sitting in Shinnecock Bay. He also realized that his bowels had let loose. It was the last thought he had before he died.

Chapter 15

Dead Men Do Tell Tales

Jake sat at his teak desk inside his dining room and looked out his window. It was late in the evening. Although he could see stars shining over the Coast Guard Station just to the southeast of his home, he could also hear the ocean waves pounding onto the barrier beach just a mile away. The pounding was fierce. He knew a storm was coming.

Jake had thought about what had happened earlier in the evening. Perhaps he should have put on his big boy pants and just gone into the Maples Bar. He could have just ignored the people he didn't like, stayed a few minutes and then left through the side door. He could never figure out why he let certain people get under his skin like this.

This year it was going to be Jillian Stark. Last year it was his old Lieutenant's admin officer Phil "refill please" Walsh. May he rest in peace.

Then, of course, there was Elizabeth Quinn. She was someone he thought about often. "Beth" is what she said he should call her. She had certainly gotten under his skin, but in a good way. She was the Historian for this little community and she had helped him last year to break open one of the most interesting cases he had ever worked on. It had everything, including homicides, Beth, missing gold treasure, shipwrecks, precious jewels and Beth. Thinking back, other than getting shot, he really had a pretty good time. She was traveling in Europe now and was on some kind of historical quest. The last and only letter he had ever received from her didn't say when or if she would ever be back. Although they hardly knew each other, for some inexplicable reason he really missed her. Rather than trying to figure it out, he simply told himself he needed to move on.

Jake's thoughts then shifted to the still-open homicide cases he had scattered on the desk in front of him. They were all pretty straightforward cases. Most were domestic related.

The others were drug related. None of them were really interesting. He pushed the folders aside and reminded himself that there would always be new homicide cases coming into the squad. He truly believed that ever since the day that Cain looked down at that rock and then at his brother Abel, things had pretty much remained the same as far as man's inhumanity to man was concerned. He knew that there would be more cases coming along soon. As it turned out, he didn't have to wait long.

Three days later, as Jake was walking into the squad room, he met Holly on her way out. Holly stopped him and said, "Hey, the boss is looking for you."

"Where is he?"

"He's in his office with the bride of Frankenstein. Door's closed. I would knock real loud if I were you. Make sure you give him time to pull his pants up." Holly rolled her eyes and then stepped into the hall.

Jake had no intention of going anywhere near the boss's office and decided to make a few case-related calls instead. He was on his third call when he looked up and saw Jillian Stark standing at his desk.

Once they made eye contact, she just pointed towards the Lieutenant's office and headed out of the squad room.

Jake finished his call, glanced around the squad room to see if Jillian had returned and then stepped into Lieutenant Blair's office.

"You wanted to see me, Lieutenant?"

"Yeah, please take a seat."

Jake took a seat at the small conference table and Blair retrieved a handwritten note from his desk. "Ok, the M.E.'s office called first thing this morning and said they had a suspicious death." He continued, "She started rattling off some scientific test results. I didn't understand a freaking thing the girl was saying. Anyway, the body was found out in your neck of the woods, you know, out in the Hamptons, so I thought you should get the case." With that Lieutenant Blair handed him the notes he had taken over the phone.

The notes said, "Sue, M.E.s Office," followed by a telephone number. Jake knew better than to ask for any more details. He took the notes and said, "Thanks, I'll get right on this." In his head he was thinking, "Really? They pay you to do this?"

Jake arrived at the Medical Examiner's office just before noon. He had called "Sue" and they had arranged to meet.

Sue was Susan Beacher and she and Jake had been friends for several years. Susan Beacher was a single mother trying to raise a 17-year-old son. Her "little boy Luke" had already gotten himself into several jams, which included shoplifting and vandalism. Last year he upped the ante to commercial burglary. He and his 18-year-old best friend had been caught inside a closed Safeway supermarket at two o'clock in the morning trying to open a 2000-pound safe with a claw hammer and wood chisel. Sue had called Jake the next morning. In between all the tears, she managed to tell him the story. This time, as opposed to the previous arrests, she left out the part about how her son had sworn to her that he was innocent and it was all a big mistake. In the end, she just wanted advice from Jake as to what she should do now that her son was sitting in a cell out at the county jail. Jake told her to hang up the phone and wait for a call. Fifteen minutes later, the most prominent defense attorney in the county called her. His first words to her were, "Jake Tucker called me. This is what I am going to do for your son."

Susan Beacher had a small office on the second floor of the Medical Examiner's building. Jake stuck his head around the corner, looked in, smiled and said, "Hey, Sue."

She stepped from around her desk and gave Jake a hug.

"So, how is he doing?" Jake asked.

"Good!" she said. "He's taking classes at the community college and he has a new girlfriend. This one is different. She only has two tattoos that I can see and calls me Ma'am. I like her." She then asked, "So, how are you doing Jake? You know, with that new Lieutenant of yours and his girlfriend."

"Wow!" said Jake. "Does everyone in the county government know what's going on in the homicide squad room?"

"Don't be ridiculous," she said. "It isn't the whole county government, Jake. It's just everyone here at the M.E.s office and the Crime Lab downstairs. Oh yeah, and everybody in the D.A.s Office next door. Other than that, I think it's a pretty well-kept secret."

Sue's sardonic wit had always made Jake smile and he loved their conversations. He just shook his head back and forth and finally asked, "So, what do you have for me?"

"Ah," she said, "you're going to like this one."

Jake followed Susan down to the cold storage area. There was an examining table in the room and a body had already been laid out. By the condition of the corpse, it was clear that the autopsy had been completed. Susan handed Jake the little jar of Vicks VapoRub she always kept in her pocket. No matter how much cleaning and ventilation there was, the smell of human body decay was always present in this room. Jake placed a small dab of the Vicks right below his nostrils and handed the jar back to Susan.

Susan said, "Ok, what we have here is a 38-year-old male..."

"Wait," said Jake. "How do you know he's 38 years old?"

"Driver's license, Jake! Now stop interrupting me." She continued, "He is a 38-year-old male that appears to have died of radiation poisoning. Technically, it's called Acute Radiation Syndrome or ARS." She added, "In addition to the CBC that we ran, there is this erythema here on the hands and arms."

Jake leaned forward to get a closer look at the red tinted skin Sue was pointing to. She said, "This is caused by the dilation of the blood capillaries. There is also evidence of damaged sebaceous glands and evidence of recent severe vomiting and diarrhea. I also found evidence of what is known as deep gamma burns. This included gamma burns on several of his internal organs. Finally, there is evidence of necrosis on the finger tips." She stopped for a moment and asked, "Any questions so far?"

He replied, "Yeah, a lot. But you keep going."

She smiled at him and continued, "There is no evidence that he breathed in or ate something radioactive."

Jake stopped her, "Now I have to ask. How do you know that?"

"Because," she said, "we took lots of tissue samples from the lungs and the entire digestive tract. Stuck them under a Geiger counter and got a zero reading. Not hard, Jake. He didn't eat it or breathe it in. The type of skin damage that is present, on top of the burned organs, makes me believe that this guy was exposed to gamma radiation. A lot of gamma radiation. In fact, I would go so far as to say that he probably picked up a high energy radioactive source and held it in his hands. That would account for the necrosis on the finger tips."

She paused and said, "And he was found sitting in his car which he had driven right into Shinnecock Bay."

Jake looked at the body and then shifted his gaze to Susan and said, "You're right. I like this one."

Chapter 16

Back At the Barn

Jack Ford had been busy over the last few days. Between his regular job, watching over his mother, and the radiation research he was doing, he barely noticed that Zabo had not been around. Since he hadn't seen Zabo's car, he assumed he must have gone back home or he was picked up by the cops on a warrant. Either way, it was good Zabo wasn't staying here anymore. Selling the stuff in the barn to someone like Patti Ball would pay off in chump change compared to what he had in mind.

Ford had finally put his hands on a Geiger counter. It took a few days, but he finally found the one he wanted on eBay and he had it shipped to his work address. It was an old CDV-715 Civil Defense Geiger counter, one of those yellow and black ones you sometimes see in the old movies. It came with a note saying it had to be calibrated properly in order to produce accurate readings. Ford really didn't care about its accuracy. He just wanted to know if there was anything in those concrete casts that was putting out radiation. He also purchased a new hasp and padlock for the barn door. No reason to take any chances and have a nosey neighbor, or worse, some asshole town building inspector, popping in through an unlocked door. Besides, he was pretty confident that Zabo wasn't coming back anytime soon.

Late one afternoon, Ford decided that he had stalled long enough and it was now time to try out the Geiger counter. He had done enough reading on radiation exposure in Wikipedia to know that time, distance and shielding were the things he needed to keep in mind while he was doing this. He knew he couldn't do anything about the distance, because he had to open the lids with his hands. But if he could just crack the lid open a little bit, and only for a few seconds, he might be able to get a quick reading on the Geiger counter.

Ford entered the back of the old Bell Telephone Company van and moved forwards towards the concrete casts. He pulled out his cell phone and took several photographs. He made sure to get close enough so that the faded writing and symbols on the casts could be seen in the final pictures. If things worked out like he hoped, he thought he might want to print one or two of these and include them in a letter he was planning to write.

Once he was finished taking his pictures, he turned on his Geiger counter and sat it on top of one of the casts. He watched the needle carefully for any sign of movement. There was none. He then moved to the cast right next to the Geiger counter, put both his hands on the concrete lid and slowly lifted one side of it up. He had raised it about 2 inches when he saw the needle move. It wasn't much. But he definitely saw it move. He lowered the lid back into place and moved the Geiger counter to the next cast. He then repeated the process with the second cast. The needle moved again. Ford stopped to think for a moment. There was probably no need to test all of these right now. He decided he would test one more and moved to the concrete cast on the end. When the Geiger counter was properly placed, he began lifting the concrete lid.

His first thought was that this lid was a lot heavier than the last two. Suddenly, he blinked his eyes twice and asked himself, "Did I just see that?"

It had happened so fast that Ford wasn't sure it had happened at all. As he was struggling with the weight of the lid, he thought he saw the needle on the Geiger counter spike to the top of the scale and then fall to "0." Once this had happened, he had instinctively dropped the concrete lid back into place. He thought to himself, "Oh, baby. This could be a really hot one."

Ford was now confident that at least three of the eight casts contained radioactive material. He also decided that the last cast he checked would be the first one he used.

Ford backed out of the van and stepped onto the floor of the barn. He then looked into the far corner and saw the lantern he had given Zabo. He also saw Zabo's suitcase still sitting on the floor.

He thought to himself, "He didn't go home. He got pulled over and locked up. Bye-bye, Zabo."

As he clicked the padlock closed on the barn door he thought to himself, "I have the Geiger counter reading and the photographs I need. All I have to do now is write a little letter."

Chapter 17

Road Work

Jake had spent his day gathering background information on Zabo Pruit. Pruit's wallet contained his driver's license, a couple of credit cards and fifty-seven dollars in cash. Jake's computer told him that Zabo Pruit had a long string of petty thefts. He also had a couple of felony arrests that had been pled down to misdemeanors. There was also an outstanding bench warrant out for him for "failure to appear" in court.

Jake spent most of the day in Southampton. He interviewed the first officer on the scene of Zabo's car accident. He followed this up with an interview of the person who made the 911 call. It turned out to be someone Jake knew.

The person who made the call was Maureen Penny. She lived on Wakeman Road which was about a half mile away from where Zabo crashed his car into the bay. Jake had met her during a cold case homicide investigation last year. She had been very helpful. Jake called ahead and arranged to meet Maureen at her house on Wakeman Road. When Jake pulled into her driveway he saw her working in her small vegetable garden. She waved and signaled him to come over to a small table and chairs that were set up under an umbrella.

They exchanged the usual pleasantries and then she said, "I read about all those old murder cases you solved last year. I could not believe that that kind of thing could happen in a small town like this. I was glad I could help, even if it was only a little."

Jake replied, "It was more than a little. Your old high school graduation party picture pointed me in the right direction. I owe you a great deal of thanks."

She looked at him and said, "And here we are again."

"Yes, here we are again. The responding officer to the accident at the bay said you may have seen something."

"Oh, I saw it all right," she said. "I had just finished walking my dog along the beach and was about to step onto the roadway when I saw this car coming over the top of the hill. The car wasn't going very fast but it was weaving from one side of the road to the other. Well, I reached down and leashed my dog. When I looked again I realized he was not going to stop. He went right through that old snow fence and plowed into the bay. He didn't get very far. Besides, you have to walk out at least 200 yards just to have the water come up to your waist. I knew he wasn't going to drown. I walked to the edge of the water and shouted at him. I saw this man with his head resting on the steering wheel like he was sleeping. I shouted at him at least two more times and he didn't respond. He didn't even move. He looked drunk to me. Anyway, that's when I used my cell phone and called 911. Then the Southampton Police arrived followed by an ambulance a couple of minutes later. That's it. That's all I saw."

Jake had been taking notes and put his pen down. He asked, "Did you see anyone else on the road or on the beach just before or even just after this happened?"

"No," she said. "That's a pretty secluded shoreline and I rarely see anyone down there."

Jake thanked her for her time and decided to head over to Southampton Hospital.

On the ride over to the hospital, he thought about what Maureen Penny had seen. It occurred to him that if Zabo was in that bad shape that he couldn't drive in a straight line or even use the brake, then he couldn't have been on the road very long. He must have come from somewhere nearby. Perhaps he came from a motel room near Lighthouse Road or maybe a nearby residence.

Jake parked his car in the hospital's parking lot and headed for the main entrance. As Jake entered the hospital, his mind was flooded with memories of last year's shooting that took place at that old Indian grave. He had killed one of the assailants and injured another, but not before one of them got a shot off at him. It had struck him on his left side and had gone straight through and exited out his back. The bad guys had turned out to be members of the Gambino crime family. He thought, "What a night that was." His mind quickly shifted to his ride home from the hospital. Beth had picked him up and…

"Sir, can I help you?" asked the receptionist.

Jake was standing in front of the hospital's information desk. He smiled and took out his Police ID and said, "I'm looking for your records room."

The receptionist pointed and said, "Down that hall and make a left. You'll see the sign on the door."

Jake entered the records room and was greeted by a pleasant young man named David. Jake identified himself as being from the Suffolk County PD's Homicide Squad and said, "I'm investigating the death of Zabo Pruit. He was in a car accident in Hampton Bays and was transported here by ambulance a few days ago. I was hoping to find out the name of the emergency room doctor who first treated him when he arrived."

David replied, "Oh, I remember that guy. He was covered in vomit and feces. Not a single contusion and not a drop of alcohol in his blood. Weird, right?"

Jake was a little surprised at this and asked, "So, you were present in the E.R. when they brought him in?"

David replied, "Oh, no, I just read all the reports from the E.R. that come in here. The Records Clerk before me, Alice Spinks, taught me that if you really want to know what's going on in the hospital, just read the reports that come in. She worked in this room for almost 40 years. She's retired now and living in North Sea."

David had moved to a file cabinet and was going through one of the drawers. "I don't think the hard copy of the E.R. paperwork has been scanned yet," he said. "It should just take me minute to find it."

As David was searching for the report, Jake suddenly had an idea. "David, have you ever seen or even heard about anyone in the hospital being treated for radiation exposure?"

David stopped his search and turned his head towards Jake. "Is that what that guy had? I knew it was something weird."

Jake said, "David, I did not say that. Now, to my question. Have you ever…."

"No," said David. "But I've only been in this job for a couple of years. You should ask Alice."

Jake asked, "Would you mind giving me her home telephone number and address?"

Ten minutes later Jake walked out of the records room with a copy of Zabo's E.R. records and Alice Spinks' telephone number.

The E.R. doctor that pronounced Zabo dead was on vacation now. Jake decided his interview could wait a few days. Jake had arranged with the Southampton PD to examine Pruit's car and pick up Pruit's personal effects including his cell phone. The car had been impounded and was now sitting in a secure fenced-in area behind the Town's police headquarters. The interior of the car smelled really bad. Between Zabo's body fluids and the rotting seaweed, the smell from the interior of the car made Jake retch. He had to open all the doors and let the car air out for a few minutes before he could search it. After an hour's search of the car, the only thing that Jake removed was a small scrap of paper that had been stuck behind the driver's side visor. It was a small handwritten note that contained only two words: "mill race."

Late that afternoon Jake found himself on Sandy Hollow Road heading north into North Sea. He had reached out to Alice Spinks earlier and she said she would be happy to meet with him. He pulled into the driveway at 231 Shore Road and was met by a very large Bernese Mountain Dog that was intent upon licking his face off. As he was petting the dog, he heard a woman's voice say, "He likes you. He doesn't greet everyone that way."

"Hi," said Jake. He started to reach for his I.D. when she said, "No need. I know who you are. I got a call from the hospital telling me that you might be contacting me. Let's step around to the back of the house and sit by the water."

As they followed the walkway around to the back of the house Jake saw that the rear of the property backed up to a small creek leading to North Sea Harbor. She pointed to a wooden picnic table sitting on a flagstone patio. They both took seats. Alice asked, "Can I get you anything, Detective? Water or coffee perhaps?"

"No, thank you," said Jake. "I do appreciate you taking the time to see me." He continued, "I was wondering if you could remember seeing or hearing about any case involving radiation exposure while you worked at the hospital?"

Alice sat in silence for a few moments and finally said, "We had an occasional cancer treatment patient come in with burns to their skin that needed to be checked. No, we didn't have any cases like that for a very long time."

Jake said, "It sounds like you did have one."

She said, "Oh, yes. A very sad case involving a little girl, but it had to be over 30 years ago."

Jake said, "Tell me about it."

She replied, "Well, I don't know how much I can remember. I had only been working at the hospital for a short time. I remember reading records about this little girl who was suffering from some kind of radiation sickness. She eventually died in the hospital. I can't tell you any more than that."

Jake asked, "Do you remember the doctor's name?"

"Oh yes," she replied. "His name was Dr. Hammond. He was with the hospital for years. I think he passed away about eight years ago."

"Do any of the existing hospital records date back that far?"

"Sure," she said. "I had a grant from the New York State Health Department many years ago that let me put about three decades worth of hospital records onto microfilm. We stopped doing that once the computer scanning became cost effective. Every once in a while I would be asked to retrieve a very old patient record so I made sure that the microfilm readers stayed running."

Jake asked, "Do you think it would be possible to search the records for this little girl, possibly by using her doctor's name?"

"Maybe," she replied. "I am pretty sure this happened in the late 1970s."

Jake said, "Next question. Do you think the hospital would do a search for these records if I asked?"

"Oh, no. Absolutely not," she said. "But my grandson David will do it for me if I ask."

Jake gave Alice his business card and asked her to call him anytime, day or night, if she or David should find out anything about the little girl. Jake checked his watch and saw that it was now close to 7:00 pm. It was time to go home.

Chapter 18

Ever Vigilant

Susan Beacher looked at the clock on the wall in her office. It was now 7:15 pm and she wanted to be home when her son Luke returned from his evening class at the community college. She had just completed her final report regarding autopsy findings for Zabo Pruit. Susan was one of those people who like to keep her draft reports on a thumb drive. This allowed her to work on many of her reports at home, which in turn, allowed her to spend more time watching over her troublesome teenage son. Now, her report on Mr. Pruit was finished and it was time to save that final report to the M.E.'s office server.

Susan opened the folder on her thumb drive and dragged the final report over to the final autopsy's folder on the server. When the computer indicated that the file had transferred properly she removed her thumb drive, threw it in her bag and shut down her computer. She grabbed her light jacket and headed for the door.

Before Susan reached the door of her office, her file had been scanned, copied and sent to a secured server in Dimona, Israel. Upon its arrival on the Israeli server, a text message was automatically generated and sent to a high-ranking member of the Mossad.

It had been long ago determined by certain high up members in the Israeli intelligence services that the historic activities surrounding Operation Apollo and other Israeli operations just like it around the world needed to be protected from disclosure. All of the efforts surrounding how and when Israel secured its original nuclear materials were considered a state secret and had to be protected at all costs. Israel had not signed the infamous Non-Nuclear Proliferation Treaty and had never acknowledged that it possessed nuclear weapons. Disclosure of the details surrounding Operation

Apollo could easily bring about international condemnation and further isolation from the international community.

Since the United States was the target of this particular theft, it was unlikely that they would support Israel in any vote or action brought forth by the United Nations Security Council. Because of all this, Israeli intelligence had taken precautions. They were well aware that the stolen uranium had been moved to a safe location on Long Island many years ago. However, over the decades they had lost two seasoned Mossad agents in an attempt to retrieve these materials.

It was decided that further retrieval attempts would not be made, but a surveillance system would be put into place to monitor both the media and medical authorities within a fifty-mile radius of where the Highly Enriched Uranium was supposed to be. During the late 1990s, Israeli intelligence operatives remotely inserted computer bots into numerous computer systems throughout Suffolk County. These were basically automated computer programs that ran over the internet. The bots had been upgraded on four separate occasions since their original installation. The latest version of the bot contained computer code that had been somewhat modeled after the Israeli Stuxnet virus that was developed in 2005 and planted within the Iranian nuclear program's computers. The damage that was done reportedly set Iran's nuclear program back by several years before the virus was finally discovered in 2010.

The bots in Suffolk County had been implanted in numerous hospitals, police departments, M.E's offices, Brookhaven National Laboratory and media outlets with the sole purpose of monitoring each system for the mention of certain words and phrases such as uranium, high enriched uranium, radiation contamination and radiation sickness. All for the purpose of giving Israeli intelligence advance warning that the uranium stolen from the NUMEC facility decades earlier had been or was about to be discovered.

Chapter 19

Devising an Ultimatum

Jack Ford sat at his small writing desk in his room while his mother slept down the hall. He was in the very same room that Yoni Levy had stayed in many years before. As he looked out his bedroom window he could see the moon reflecting off the little creek behind his house.

"That's the way they will come," he thought to himself. "If they ever find out that it is me, that is the direction the cops will come from. They won't come from the street."

Jack Ford had been thinking about his plan for several days. It was now time to start the old ball rolling. His initial thought was to bury all eight of the concrete casts from the barn just above the high tide mark at eight different Hampton's beaches. He would start at the Ponquogue Beach in Hampton Bays and work east to Asparagus Beach off Atlantic Avenue in Amagansett. He would surround each of the casts with explosives, courtesy of his former employer, and set a timer to go off in the middle of the afternoon on a beautiful summer day.

It would be the kind of summer day that the Hamptons are known for. Sunshine, beaches, blankets and bikinis as far as the eye can see. He knew that the actual explosions probably wouldn't kill many people. Killing a lot of people was not his goal. His goal was to spread radioactive contamination just as far as he could.

He truly believed that it would never even occur to anyone to check for radiation after the explosion. That was the beauty of the plan. All of those people running from the beach would spread the contamination to their cars and maybe even their homes. Every cop and EMT that showed up to help the blast victims would also help spread the contamination. They would most likely drive the cop vehicles right through the contamination on the beach and drag the stuff right down every main road all the way to the local hospital. With any luck, the incoming high tide would come in, pick up some of the radioactive debris, and perhaps spread it up and down the entire beach.

Ford looked over at the little alarm clock next to his bed and saw that it was 2:00 am. What occupied his thoughts now was the price. The price the idiots running the government would have to pay him not to do this. The price the idiots in government would pay not to have contamination spread all over their precious beaches and streets. Ford expected that this might even force the government to close the beaches for decades. How much would that cost the idiots in beloved lost tax dollars?

Ford expected them not to believe any threat that he made. Any threatening call or letter would probably be paid lip service and mostly ignored. He had to get their attention before any serious negotiations could occur. He decided on a four step approach. First, a call to the County Executive's Office telling them what was going to happen and also that they should expect a letter with more details as to how many people were going to die. Second, the letter itself would repeat the threat, but it would also contain a little art. Perhaps a picture or two of all eight of the concrete casts with some of the writing and symbols clearly visible in the pictures. That would get their attention. Third, and this was Ford's favorite part of the plan, another call to the County Executive's Office would be made telling them exactly where they could find one of the buried casts. Fourth, they would find the device, disarm it and know for sure that the threat was real. They would also know that there were seven more of these bad boys just like the one they found. Now they could start talking about real money. Five million dollars in cash sounded good to Jack Ford. With that final thought, he reached for the pen and paper on his desk.

Chapter 20

Knowing What You Don't Know

Jake started his day by dropping off Zabo's cell phone to the crime lab technicians to see if they could somehow bypass the passcode. They were not hopeful, but they did say they would give it a try.

An hour later the crime lab called and said they had gotten into the phone. It turns out that they didn't break the passcode. Instead, they found the passcode.

It seems that Google has a list of the top 25 most common passcodes that people use for their computers and cell phones. Zabo used passcode "123456." It was number one on the Google list.

Jake had picked up Zabo's phone and returned to his office a little after noon. He finally had a chance to sit down and eat his lunch at his desk. He had been looking forward to this moment since he got out of bed that morning. This was his special lunch day.

One day each month Jake treated himself to a very large BLT hero from the local deli. This thing was a real heart clogger. It had about a pound of bacon on it and was smothered in mayonnaise. As he ate his hero, trying not to get bacon grease and mayonnaise on his shirt, he began examining the incoming and outgoing calls on Zabo's cell phone and making notes.

He had been at this for about 10 minutes when he sensed somebody standing over his desk. He looked up to see Jillian Stark staring down at him with a very disapproving look on her face. "Is that evidence?" she asked.

Since there was an open evidence envelope from Southampton PD sitting on Jake's desk the answer was pretty self-evident. Jake decided against pointing out the rhetorical nature of her question and simply said, "I don't know yet. It might contain a lead that…"

She interrupted him and said, "You need a search warrant to look at that phone."

Jake slowly put Zabo's cell phone down on his desk and sighed. He replied, with just the right amount of condescension and frustration in his voice, "Jillian, the Fourth Amendment right against unreasonable searches and seizures does not apply to dead people. Now, please go find some other flock to shepherd. I'm trying to solve a homicide and I do not have the time to instruct inexperienced detectives on basic constitutional law issues."

Jake broke his eye contact with Jillian, picked up the cell phone and continued making notes. Jillian turned on her heels and headed straight for the Lieutenant's office. When Jake heard the office door slam he looked up to see Holly Gilpin sitting two desks away with a big smile on her face. She mouthed a single word to him. It was, "Run."

Jake knew that he had a choice of explaining himself for the next hour in the Lieutenant's office, in front of the Lieutenant's girlfriend, or leaving and getting some police work done. He just wanted to sit at his desk and examine the call logs, contacts, and photographs on Zabo's phone. It wasn't going to happen. The bullshit was going to get in the way again. He quickly packed up Zabo's cell phone and his notes and the remains of his sandwich and headed for the squad room exit. He wasn't absolutely sure, but he thought he heard someone shout his name just as he hit the door.

Jake had determined that there were two outgoing calls made from Zabo's phone just a few hours before he died. One was to Zabo's wife, Jeannine Pruit. The other was to a low-level criminal by the name of Patrick Ball. Jake's computer had indicated that Patrick Ball, AKA Patti Ball, ran an asbestos transportation company in the county. Jake had Zabo's home address from his driver's license and started heading towards his home in Patchogue. The M.E.'s office had let him know that Jeannine Pruit, accompanied by her brother, had been in late yesterday afternoon to identify the body.

Jake swung his unmarked police car into an empty parking space at 200 River Avenue, Patchogue. It was a large apartment complex, but Jake had no problem finding the right apartment number.

Jake rung the door bell and then stepped aside. Stepping to the side was an old habit. He didn't like the thought of someone standing on the other side of the door with a shotgun in their hands. Fortunately, most doors are made of metal these days, which might make his precaution seem a little unnecessary. Jake heard footfalls approaching the door. He reached for his I.D. When the door opened, he saw a woman in her 30's facing him with a glass in her hand. Her long brown hair was disheveled and her eyes were bloodshot. Jake knew the glass was filled with Scotch. He knew the smell well. Jake asked, "Mrs. Pruit?"

She replied, "Yes."

Jake said, "I am Detective Jake Tucker. First, let me say that I am sorry for your loss. I am sure that this is a difficult time for you and your family. I have been assigned to examine the circumstances surrounding your husband's passing. May I come in for a minute?"

"Sure, come on in." Jake noticed the slurring of her words and realized that Mrs. Pruit might be drunk.

Her unsteady walk to a chair just a few feet away confirmed Jake's worry. He decided to leave the front door open and remain standing in the doorway. Jake began by asking, "Mrs. Pruit, can you tell me what your husband did for a living?"

She replied, "He didn't do anything for a living. He got fired."

"Okay," said Jake. "Can you tell me what job he got fired from?"

"Sure," she said. "He worked at the Home Depot on Sunrise Highway."

Jake asked, "Can you tell me what he did there?"

"Sure," she said. "He stole things. In fact, he stole something from the store every single day he worked there.

That's what my dead husband did for a living. He stole things." She continued, "Now there is no paycheck, no insurance money, no money for a funeral and my rent is due in six days."

Jake had many more questions but thought it best to cut the interview short. "Just a couple more questions, Mrs. Pruit. When was the last time you saw your husband alive?"

She said, "About a week ago. He showed up late one night and I told him the cops were here looking for him. They said they had a warrant. When I told him that, he packed a suitcase and took off. He said he would call me."

"Did he call you?"

"Yeah, he called me. He said he was staying with his friend Ford for a few days until things calmed down."

Jake asked, "Do you know where this friend lives?

"Nope, not a clue," she said.

Jake asked, "Is Ford his first name or his last name?"

"Last." she said.

"Do you know Ford's first name?" asked Jake.

She shook her head no and took a long drink from her glass.

Jake said, "Well, I want to thank you for your time. Here is my card. Should you remember anything else that you think is important, please call me." With that Jake left the apartment and headed for his car.

Just before he started his car he checked his cell phone for messages. There were six. All six were from the Lieutenant's office number. He decided he would call the Lieutenant's office phone and leave a message for him after working hours. That had worked well for him with past bad bosses. The conversation normally went something like, "But boss, I called you back and left you a message. You must have been gone for the day."

Thirty minutes later Jake pulled into the parking lot of the District Attorney's Office. He had a meeting scheduled with Detective John Flynn who was assigned to the D.A.'s Environmental Crime Unit. John Flynn knew a lot about radiation and Jake was in desperate need of a quick education on the subject. John had been with the Department for over twenty years. He was a former Army Ranger and had spent a great deal of his career in the Emergency Services Unit. He did a lot of different jobs there including S.W.A.T., heavy rescue, bombs and hazardous materials. It was his hazardous materials training that landed him in the Environmental Crime Unit. That and the fact that he was the only living Medal of Honor winner in the Department. In fact, he could have gone to any detective squad he wanted to. He chose the Environmental Crimes Unit.

As Jake was walking into the D.A.'s Office he thought back to the first time he had met John.

It was back when Jake had just made detective and he had been assigned to the 3rd Precinct Detective Squad. He had just gotten home from a day shift when he got a call on his home phone from the precinct. It was the desk Sergeant, who said that Jake was to immediately bag up all the clothes and shoes he wore at the precinct that day. After bagging them up, he was to immediately take a shower and then bring the bag back to the precinct.

When Jake arrived back at the precinct, he found that all hell had broken loose. Media satellite trucks were lined up bumper-to-bumper up and down the entire main avenue. It looked like every major new station from New York City was there including ABC, NBC, CBS, CNN and Fox News. He saw the Red Cross setting up one of their large tents in a nearby parking lot. There were Emergency Service Units all around the precinct. A heavy security corridor had been set up and he could see blue uniforms everywhere. Jake finally made his way through security barriers and then headed for the employee parking lot. A bunch of precinct personnel were standing around. Some of them had still their bags of clothes in their hands.

Jake spotted his Lieutenant and walked over to him. "What the hell is going on?" Jake asked. "I just left two hours ago and everything was fine."

The Lieutenant said, "Come here. A picture is worth a thousand words."

Jake followed the Lieutenant to the far rear corner of the parking lot. From this vantage point, you could just see the rear of the precinct about 200 yards away. The Lieutenant said, "See the picnic table? See the thing on the picnic table?"

Jake squinted in an effort to better understand what he was seeing. What he saw was a plastic or glass bowl with a green liquid inside, sitting on top of the very spot where he usually ate his lunch. The part that Jake had difficulty processing was the fact that the green liquid was glowing.

Jake finally asked, "What the hell is that? Is it what I think it is?"

"I don't know," said the Lieutenant. "Somebody walked into the precinct carrying that thing and then all hell broke loose. One of the desk guys took it from the lobby and put it on the picnic table in the back. He's getting checked over by the EMTs right now on the other side of the building. The last that I heard was that the building has been quarantined and they called everyone in from the day shift. Nobody can come out and only E.S. guys and Environmental Crime guys are going in." He pointed and said, "That's the Environmental Crime guys going in now. That big guy is John Flynn."

As Jake would find out later, the persons who had brought the glowing liquid into the precinct were a very frightened mother and her 10-year-old son named Johnny. Johnny had told the Environmental Crime detectives that he had been riding his bicycle on Chestnut Street. At the corner of Chestnut and Pine Streets was an empty lot that had a path that you could ride your bike on to cut through to the next block. When he was riding on the path, he had seen two silver canisters, so he got off his bike so he could get a close look at them. Each was about 18 inches long and each had the word "Radon" stenciled on their sides in black letters. Some other kids, that he did not know, came along on their bikes and took one of the canisters with them. Johnny said he unscrewed the cap off of his canister and found a tube of green liquid inside. He left the empty canister in the lot and took the green tube home with him. He said he then broke the tube open at home and poured the contents into one of his mother's glass bowls.

Then his mother came home from work. Instead of dialing 911, the mother loaded Johnny and the glowing bowl into her car and headed for the local police precinct. Now Johnny was wearing a paper suit and was sitting in an interview room with both of his parents, being interviewed by Detective John Flynn and his partner.

It was not until several months later that Jake heard the rest of the story directly from John Flynn. Flynn told him that after he and his partner interviewed Johnny, they put on their safety equipment and tested their Geiger counters. Their plan was to begin a radiation survey in the now-evacuated lobby and slowly work their way through the double entry glass doors at the rear. From there they would slowly work their way to the source sitting on top of the picnic table.

As the Environmental Crime guys were getting ready to make their first entry, the E.S. Commanding Officer had his hands full. He had E.S. units monitoring the air all around the precinct's perimeter for any sign of radioactivity. He had also dispatched additional Emergency Service personnel to the empty lot where the Radon canisters had been originally found. That area may have still contained contamination and needed to be secured as a crime scene. He was also working with other county officials in preparation for an emergency network broadcast to be made regarding the missing second canister and the unknown children who had removed it from the empty lot. The County Health Commissioner was now preparing the proper orders to allow a public health emergency to be called within the impacted neighborhood. Most importantly, the E.S. commanding officer had opened up a communications channel with Brookhaven National Laboratory. The laboratory was located approximately 30 miles to the east of the precinct. They had a specialized team of physicists and technicians on standby and were ready to respond if necessary.

Flynn said that he and his partner started surveying all of the floor space, walls, chairs and tables in the lobby and that their Geiger counters were capable of detecting even trace amounts of radiation. There appeared to be no radiation contamination in the lobby so they moved to the double-doored vestibule. According to Flynn, the outside light had faded and the glow from the picnic table had gotten brighter. Once they entered the vestibule, their Geiger counters began to register the presence of radioactive material. The readings got stronger as they moved through the vestibule and entered the rear yard area of the precinct. Then, inexplicably, both Geiger counters dropped to zero. Flynn had explained that this can happen when a radiological source is so powerful that the instrument gets overloaded. Usually, the needle on the display will peg to the top of the scale and fall back to zero. If you are not watching carefully, the action can be missed. Flynn said that neither he nor his partner had seen the needles on their instruments peg out, but they were not going to take any chances.

Flynn likes to tell people, "You have to know what you don't know," and he knew he had reached the end of his knowledge when it came to measuring radiation. Both he and his partner returned to the precinct lobby and met with the E.S. Commanding Office. Flynn recommended that the Brookhaven National Laboratory emergency response team be called in immediately.

According to Flynn, it took the Brookhaven National Laboratory Team 30 minutes to respond. It took another 30 minutes for them to be fully briefed and to set up their equipment. A team of three physicists wearing safety equipment and carrying state-of-the-art Geiger counters slowly moved through the same path taken by John and his partner. The team moved through the vestibule and slowly worked their way right up to the picnic table. John said that, from his position in the lobby, he could see that all three of the physicists were having what appeared to be a rather animated discussion while standing right next to the glowing liquid.

Suddenly one of the physicists picked up the glowing bowl and carried it right back into the precinct lobby. He put it down on the reception counter and said, "Glow stick."

At least three different people in the lobby said "What?" at the same time.

The physicist repeated, "It's a glow stick. The kind you get at the camping store. They cost about two bucks. When you break one open and pour it into a bowl it looks just like this."

John Flynn says it was at that point that his partner had turned to him and said, "Time to talk to Johnny again."

Little Johnny stood tall, stayed strong and stuck to his story for about two minutes before the tears came. In the end, there were no silver canisters marked Radon. There were no other children on their bicycles. There was only Johnny riding his bike to the camping store on Sunrise Highway and buying a glow stick. Johnny wasn't allowed to ride his bike on the Sunrise Highway and when his mother came home and saw the glow stick's contents glowing in one of her salad bowls he felt he had to come up with a story…and he did.

As Flynn likes to tell people, it may have cost the taxpayers a hundred thousand dollars that night, but the memories were priceless.

Jake was now sitting across from John Flynn's desk. They had just finished filling their coffee cups and swapping the latest rumors from headquarters when John said, "I hear you have a real interesting corpse next door."

Jake asked, "Is there anything that you don't actually hear about?"

"They needed a Geiger counter to use during the autopsy. I said sure…but tell me why, and that is how I found out about your corpse."

Jake said, "John, I don't know diddly squat about radiation. What can you tell me?"

John replied, "First, I am not an expert. Those people are out at the National Lab. I can hook you up with someone if you want. If you want an opinion as to what you're looking at I will be happy to offer one."

"Talk to me, John," Jake said.

"Okay," John began. "The fact that there was no radiation inside or on the outside of the body is important."

Jake interrupted, "Wait a minute; the M.E. said he had burns on some of his internal organs. That means there is radiation there right."

"No, that's not right," said John. "Those burns are deep gamma burns caused by gamma rays. The rays go right through you and do a lot of damage, but leave no radiation behind. The only thing they leave behind is a lot of dead and dying cells. Did you ever hear about what happened in Goiânia, Brazil?"

"No," said Jake.

"Well, it may go a long way in helping you understand what you have here," said John.

John took a sip of coffee and began relating the story. He said, "The incident happened in 1987. Several men had removed a teletherapy machine from an abandoned cancer treatment facility. It was eventually taken to a scrap metal yard and sold. The individuals who had removed the machine pried it open and removed the small steel cylinder containing the radioactive source. One particular individual spent a great deal of time working on that cylinder. His name was Alves and he finally managed to pry open the cylinder's aperture window with a screw driver. It cost him several fingers and one amputated arm. Inside this canister was a highly radioactive cesium chloride, which is cesium salt made with the isotope Cesium-137. The workers had no idea what they were dealing with. All they knew was that had this material in the form of a powder that glowed. The glowing material was taken to several different homes where children were exposed. One little six-year-old girl, Leide was her name, applied the glowing powder to her body and some of the powder had fallen onto a sandwich she was eating." John paused for a moment and then continued, "Here is the important part. The child consumed radioactive material that was putting out a tremendous amount of radioactive beta particles. Her body became truly radioactive. Place a Geiger counter next to her and watch the needle go up. As opposed to your corpse. Put a Geiger counter next to him and nothing happens. Your guy was probably exposed to one helluva powerful gamma source."

"What happened to the little girl?"

"ARS, she lasted 30 days." He continued, "Jake, I don't think you're getting this. One hundred and thirty thousand people had to be screened in that community, entire buildings were demolished, 250 people were found with contamination, and four people died. Jake, do you know how much Cesium-137 was in that cylinder?"

"No," said Jake.

"Just over 3 ounces," said John.

They both looked at each other for several seconds and then Jake said, "Body count's not done yet, is it?"

After they refilled their coffee cups Jake asked, "What do you suggest I focus on?"

John replied, "Obviously, you need to find the source. It would also be helpful to know when his ARS began. If it began a day or two before he died, as I said earlier, you may be looking at a very powerful radioactive source."

Jake said, "Okay, but where do they come from? What are they used for? How does a guy like Zabo Pruit get hold of one of these things?"

John said, "As to your last question, I don't know. He could have stolen it or stumbled onto it. As to what they're used for, there are all sorts of scientific, medical and industrial uses. Hell, they use them in x-ray machines that check the quality of welds on pipes. As far as the isotope itself, it could be something like Iodine-131, Iridium-192 or even Cobalt-60. As your corpse probably found out, these things are hard to handle if you don't know what you are doing."

Jake checked his watch and realized he had been talking with John Flynn for over two hours. "Okay," Jake said. "I have one last question. What can you tell me about Patti Ball?"

John pushed back from his desk and laughed out loud. "My God, Patti Ball. What a character!"

"So you know him then?" asked Jake.

"Oh, yeah," said John. " I have run into him several times. He runs an asbestos transportation company out east. Word is he moves a lot of stolen heavy equipment. I heard he just got out of the county jail a couple of weeks ago. He was doing 90 days for passing a bad check. He did his last 30 days of his sentence on the county honor farm. To show you what a real wheeler-dealer this guy is, he supposedly arrived at the honor farm and it was really overcrowded. Ball had to sleep on a cot in a drafty hallway. He made friends with a guy who was also doing 30 days. But this guy's sentence was 30 days or a 500-dollar fine. He couldn't pay the fine so he had to do the 30 days. This guy also had one of the best bunks on the honor farm. Patti called his secretary, had her go to the court house and pay this guy's fine. The guy got out the next day and Patti took his bunk. That's Patti Ball."

Jake said goodbye to John Flynn and headed to his car. Once in the car he decided to check his cell phone again. He was hoping to get a call from Alice Spinks or her grandson David regarding the old hospital records. There was no message from either of them, but there were two more voice mails from his Lieutenant. Jake turned his cell phone off and thought to himself, "This is going to get very ugly."

Chapter 21

Threat Sent

Jack Ford sat in his room and stared at his not-yet-mailed letter to the County Executive's office. He hoped they liked the pictures he included. He had made his initial threat call that morning from a prepaid throw-away phone he had purchased at a convenience store. The person on the other end of the phone didn't seem really concerned. He just kept asking Ford to repeat things.

Ford had actually purchased two phones, both with cash. He had already destroyed the first phone after he made his call this morning. He was saving the unused phone for his next two calls. The first one would be to the County Executive telling her where to dig. The other call would be to a local TV station telling them what, where and when to film. The public should know what is going on, he felt, so they can judge our beloved government leaders accordingly.

Ford had picked a remote mailbox to use on the North Road in Mattituck. He wanted to be sure there were no ATM machines with cameras or video surveillance devices anywhere near him when he mailed his letter. He had taken other precautions too. Whenever he needed electronic parts or batteries he would spread his purchases over a wide geographical area and shop at many different stores. One of his favorites was a large CVS drugstore at the west end of the county that had a large selection of old-fashioned battery operated clock radios and alarm clocks that were perfect for his needs.

He had remembered a famous murder case in the news from a few years back where a teenage girl went missing. Her boyfriend had joined one of the search teams and actually discovered her body during the search. In fact, he had found various parts of her body because the murderer had cut her up and placed the parts into several separate trash bags. Five days later the boyfriend was arrested for the murder. The police had found a surveillance tape at a local 7/11 that showed the boyfriend buying a big box of trash bags at two o'clock in the morning on the very day the girlfriend disappeared. Since just about every store Ford went to had surveillance cameras, he made sure that he wore a baseball cap and kept his head down whenever he made a parts purchase.

Ford figured that the high and mighty would get his letter in about three days. It would take another two days for all the right experts to tell the County Executive that she might have a problem. At the same time he would expect all the cops to start gearing up. First thing they're going to do, he thought, is start looking under every rock for a terrorist. Then the feds will join them and they can all join hands and look for terrorists under rocks together.

As Ford drove towards Mattituck, he thought about the utter chaos that would occur when the idiots actually dug up his device and found that there really was radioactive material. He would love to see the looks on their faces. He decided that he should only bury one device now. He knew that once they found the first device that they would saturate every beach in the county with cops holding shovels. If they didn't pay up, he could always plant one or more of his devices later. Perhaps much later like next Christmas or even next summer. He was having too much fun and was in no hurry.

Ford still hadn't decided where the best beach was to bury his first device. As he thought about it, the most crowded beach might not be the best beach. He started thinking about all those rich, famous and powerful people who have summer mansions in East Hampton. There was Alec Baldwin, Beyonće, Robert Downey, Jr., DeNiro, George Soros and Carl Icahn. Icahn's 7-acre estate was worth $40 million dollars alone. Ford kept wondering what would happen to the property values in that little burg if the beaches were closed for say 50 years and all of the main roads were contaminated with radiation? If a device was found buried on Asparagus Beach, how many of the rich and famous would be calling government officials the next day telling them to fix this at any cost? Ford thought to himself, "I bet some of those very important and beautiful people might even be willing to pay the five million themselves."

When Ford returned home that evening, he immediately checked the new padlock he had put on the barn's door. He was worried that Zabo might return at any time and might try to let himself in. He didn't see Zabo's car, but he didn't want to take any chances. After Ford checked the barn he went into his house and sat down at his computer. He needed to check the weather for the next few nights. He needed to visit Asparagus Beach and he was looking for an overcast night with absolutely no moon or stars shining. A rainy night would be good. A little fog would even be better.

Chapter 22

Cold Cases

Several days had gone by and Jake still had not heard anything from Southampton Hospital. He was beginning to suspect that that lead was going to be a dead end.

He did finally have a long talk with his Lieutenant regarding Jillian Stark. The Lieutenant insisted that Jake treat his administrative assistant with more respect. Jake had responded with, "It's all just a big misunderstanding and if I inadvertently insulted Jillian in any way I sincerely apologize." That seemed to have placated the Lieutenant for at least the short term.

Jake had attempted to download all the photos off Zabo's cell phone onto his office computer. It turns out there was only one. The photo was a little blurry. Jake wondered if Zabo's hand had been shaking when he took it. He wasn't sure what he was looking at so he decided to email a copy to his friend John Flynn. He also found that Zabo had emailed a copy of the photograph to Patti Ball.

It was just after lunch when Alice Spinks finally called. She said, "Detective Tucker, I believe my grandson David has located the information that you were looking for. He actually found it two days ago, but I wanted to see it myself first before I called. I know that it's a very old case, but I still feel the need to protect a patient's personal medical records even when they are deceased."

Jake replied, "I understand completely and I don't want you to do anything that makes you feel uncomfortable. How about I just ask you some questions about the little girl's death and you tell me what you can?"

Alice replied, "That should work. Go ahead and ask away. Oh, by the way, the little girl's name was Betsy Vail"

"Okay," said Jake. "What caused Betsy's death?"

She replied, "Betsy died of Acute Radiation Syndrome."

“Was there any sign of radiation burns?”

“None mentioned in the file,” replied Alice.

Jake then asked, “Is there any mention as to how she became exposed to radiation? Was she being treated for cancer or have an accident involving x-rays?”

There was a pause and then Alice replied, “It says, and I am quoting now, that the source of her ARS has not been determined.”

“Is there any indication that an autopsy was done?”

“No,” she replied. “The file says her body was released to the Scott Funeral Home in Hampton Bays the day after she passed away.”

Jake asked, “So she lived in Hampton Bays?”

“Yes,” said Alice. “The file says she was a student at the Hampton Bays Elementary School.”

“Can you tell me where she lived? It’s been close to 40 years, the house may not even exist anymore.”

She said, “Well…I’m not sure about you knocking on someone’s door to ask about their dead child. Some wounds never heal, you know.”

“Alice, there has been another radiation death that appears to have a few things in common with Alice’s case. Right now my priority is to make sure that no one else gets sick. That is why I need your help on this.”

There was a long pause and then she said, “My grandson told me about the Pruit case. Okay, do you have a pen?”

Jake had left police headquarters over an hour ago and was now driving slowly down Oak Lane in Hampton Bays. He was looking for number 14. His plan was to find Betsy Vail’s old house and take a few photos of any of license plates that might be visible from the street. He would also take photos of some of the neighbors’ license plates. Jake had experience at investigating cold cases and he knew that a little computer research as to property ownership and some current car registration data would go a long way in telling him which neighbors lived here during the time Betsy Vail got sick. He also liked to know a little about any person he was about to interview. This was especially if they were wanted or had a history of violent behavior. Jake was heading south on Oak Lane when he spotted number 14 on his right. There were no cars in the driveway but the lawn had been recently cut. Also, today was obviously trash pickup day in the neighborhood and there was an empty can with its lid off sitting on the side of the road in front of the house. Jake drove to the very end of the lane which dead-ended at Smith Creek and then turned around and headed back the way he came. He made a left onto the street just past number 14. There were vehicles in driveways on both sides of the street. He used his cell phone camera to shoot all of the license plates he could see.

Jake would run both the plates and the properties from his home computer later in the evening. That should provide him with what he needed to start interviewing any possible neighbors in the morning. He planned to follow that up with an unannounced visit to Patti Ball.

Jake decided to stop at the Starbucks in town for a nice Grande dark roast. He had just settled in to one of their comfy chairs when his cell phone rang. The screen showed the number for John Flynn.

"Hey, John!" Jake said. "Did you get the photo I sent to you?"

"Yeah," said John. "That's why I called. Can you tell me where this was taken?"

Jake replied, "No idea, I got it off of my corpse's cell. Is it anything interesting?"

"Oh yeah. It's real interesting. Those cylinders in the picture are concrete casts with concrete lids. We sometimes call them pigs. Sometimes they're lined with lead. They have one purpose and one purpose only and that is to keep the big bad evil Genie in the bottle. Look, some types of radiation you can be shielded from with a piece of paper. Other types you can be shielded with a simple book. Then there is the bad stuff that puts out heavy duty gamma rays like we talked about the other day. That stuff needs to be stored and transported in the very things you have in your picture. Any questions so far?"

"No," said Jake. "Keep talking."

Flynn continued, "Listen, should you find these things you can't go anywhere near them without a Geiger counter in your hand or a radiation pager on your belt and make sure you call for an E.S. unit immediately. Based upon what you told me about the condition of your corpse, you may be looking at a lethal dose of radiation in just a couple of minutes of exposure. It may even come down to seconds if the source is hot enough."

Jake asked, "So you think this could be bad?"

Flynn replied, "No, I think it could be really bad. Let me put it this way. You know how a 45-70 rifle bullet will go right through your bullet proof vest, exit through your spine and split the engine block in the car behind you…it's worse than that."

Jake said, "So, you think it's time that I push this thing upstairs?"

"I would at least fill in your boss, just to cover your ass." Flynn paused for a second on the phone and asked, "Are you getting close?"

Jake replied, "I don't know yet. I have some leads."

"Stop by my office tomorrow," Flynn said. "I'll give you a radiation pager to wear and I'll show you how it works."

Jake finished his call with Flynn and went over the day's events in his mind while he finished his coffee. He thought it was funny that he wasn't worried about getting exposed to radiation, but he was worried about exposing what he knew so far to his boss. The Lieutenant would invariably discuss it with his paramour and then bye-bye case. She will give Blair at least five reasons why he needs to get this case out of the homicide squad, he thought, and every one of those reasons will scare the shit out of him.

Chapter 23

Threat Received

Jack Ford was correct about the government's reaction to his initial threatening telephone call. It was just one of several threat-related calls that had been logged in that day. One of the threatening calls was a direct threat to the life of the County Executive's cat. Another threatened to contaminate all of the County's drinking water supply which, of course, was impossible since the County's drinking water supply was contained in an aquifer well below the surface of the ground and spread over 2,373 square miles. At the end of the day the threat log was reviewed by a mid-level staffer in the County Executive's office who then summarized all of the threat information and passed it on to the County Police Department through the usual liaison channels.

There would be little or no follow up regarding the threatening calls received that day.

The County received Ford's letter several days later. Ever since the anthrax scares there had been a formalized procedure for handling any type of threatening mail. Ford's letter and the accompanying photograph were immediately placed into a see-through plastic envelope and placed into a special mail bin labeled "Threatening Letters." Ford's letter wasn't the only one in the bin. At the end of the day the threatening letters were reviewed again by a mid-level staffer. Unfortunately, it was a different mid-level staffer than the one that had reviewed the threatening telephone call log earlier in the week. The letter and accompanying photograph were again passed on to the County Police Department through the usual liaison channels.

The uniqueness of the threat described in Ford's letter combined with the photograph and the threatening call information was enough to pique the interest of Detective

Christine Hall in the Police Department's Intelligence Division. Although a unique threat didn't necessarily mean a viable threat, she nonetheless had a bad feeling about this one. She immediately scanned both items, being careful not to disturb any possible latent prints. After reading the letter over several times she finally decided that it would be worthwhile to find someone who could explain to her what she was looking at in the photograph. She emailed the photograph to the County Police Department's detective assigned to the Joint Terrorism Task Force in New York City. She also picked up her desk phone and dialed the extension for Emergency Services.

It was late afternoon by the time Detective Hall dropped off the letter and picture at the crime lab. As she was leaving the building her cell phone rang. Her caller ID didn't show a number which usually indicated another cop was calling her. When she answered a male voice said, "Detective Hall, my name is Bob Morse. I'm one of the supervising FBI agents here at the task force. I wanted to talk to you about the photograph you emailed in this morning. It has caused quite a stir here. Can you tell me where you got the photo?"

Detective Hall's mind raced. She had expected the call to come from her department's representative. It wasn't him. It was an FBI agent. She knew immediately that her initial instinct had been correct and that she was now sitting on a very big problem. She ignored his question and asked, "Can you tell me what those things are in the photograph?"

He replied, "Well, it would help if you gave me a little more background regarding the photo."

Detective Hall was getting pissed off now and said, "Hey, this isn't my first rodeo with you guys. Now, we both know that we both have information. You start, or this conversation is over."

There was a long pause at the other end of the telephone and finally Agent Morse said. "They are known as pigs. They are concrete casts used to store and transport radiological isotopes. This particular type was primarily used by government contractors back in the 1960s and 1970s. The lettering on the side of containers is barely visible in the photo but we think there is a chance that you're looking at containers that, at least at some point in time, held two different kinds of isotopes. One is bad, the other is very bad."

He stopped talking, took a breath and said, "Your turn."

Detective Hall replied, "The picture came in yesterday to the County Executive's office. There's a letter that came along with it. The letter and photograph are at our crime lab right now. We also had a threatening phone call about four days ago. The caller alluded to the fact that a letter would be forthcoming and that we had better pay attention."

She paused for a moment and said, "Based upon what you have told me, if there are isotopes in any of those containers, we could have a very viable threat on our hands. Am I correct in this assessment?"

Morse replied, "You are. Can you send me a copy of the letter?"

She said, "I have to get back to my office first. Give me 30 minutes."

"Email it to the following address," Morse said.

Detective Hall copied down the email address, hung up the phone and dialed her boss's number.

At 10 o'clock that evening, a young man got off the elevator at the top floor of the H. Lee Dennison county office building. This floor housed the offices of the County Executive. By coincidence, it was the same mid-level staffer who had passed on Ford's threatening letter to the Police Department. He had received a call thirty minutes earlier telling him to go to the office and prepare the main conference room for an emergency meeting and that the County Executive would be arriving a few minutes after 10 o'clock. He was also to expect the Police Commissioner, the Health Commissioner and members of their staffs. He was told to ensure that the conference table was set up for twenty people and that bottled water was available for all of the attendees. He was also told to ensure that all of the window curtains were drawn. His final function during this meeting was to take detailed notes so that an accurate record of the meeting could be memorialized.

Two hours later, all of the main players were gathered around the County Executive's conference table and were offering their final assessments. The initial briefing had been conducted by Detective Christine Hall of the Intelligence Division. However, the star of the show was clearly Dr. Bruce Koskof, who had been brought to the meeting by the E.S. Commanding Officer. Dr. Koskof was from Brookhaven National Laboratoy's Radiological Assistance Program. This group of physicists and technicians were commonly known as the R.A.P. team and had advised local county officials on radiological matters several times over the last few decades.

Dr. Koskof began to speak. "If I understand the facts as they stand now, we have an individual who is threatening to explode eight casts that may or may not contain Highly Enriched Uranium and Cobalt-60. He or she has threatened to detonate these items on eight different beaches along the southern shore of the Hamptons. It is also my understanding that he or she has made no demands as of yet."

He continued, "Now, as to the first issue. If I may borrow a phrase from our law enforcement partners in the room, that phrase being 'a gun is always to be considered loaded.' Just because you can't see the bullets doesn't mean the weapon isn't lethal. I suggest you treat these casts the same way you would any other weapon. Now, as to the possible consequences. If the casts do contain radiological material and if the casts are blown up there will be some initial air contamination in the form of suspended particles. These particles will eventually fall to the ground, hence the term fallout. If breathed in, these particles could cause significant health issues. How long those particles remain suspended in the air and how far they travel will be dependent on several factors including the wind speed and even humidity. Most of the radioactive debris will be confined to the initial blast zone. That zone, of course, will be determined by the size of the explosion. Your letter writer is quite correct about the contamination being spread by the fleeing public and incoming emergency responders."

He continued, "However, the situation could be worse. If we were dealing with an isotope such as Cesium-137, it would be much more difficult to control the spread of contamination due to the insidious nature of the material. In this case, the radioactive debris should be in large enough pieces to hinder migration caused by the natural elements such as wind and rain runoff. However, I must be honest with you, I need to think about what would happen if a contaminated section of beach was located below the high tide mark. I will have to get back to you on that one. Because of the presence of Cobalt-60, a very heavy gamma emitter, it may be too dangerous to send people into the area for remediation purposes. You may have to resort to remotes to do the cleanup for you. That would be very costly and very time consuming. If you want more information on this I can refer you to specific studies conducted at the Fukushima disaster site in Japan."

He went on, "As to blast victim triage, you are going to be facing a problem with those who have blast debris imbedded in their skin. The only known case of that happening in the U.S. was when the SLI research reactor in Idaho Falls, Idaho had an excursion in early1961. Excursion being a fancy word used at the time for a big explosion. In that situation the actual reactor exploded and two workers were killed instantly by the blast. A third worker was still alive and was lying on the reactor room floor. He was covered in core material that had been released from the reactor vessel. After several rescue attempts, the first responders managed to recover the victim and get him into an ambulance. He had radioactive core material embedded in his skin which resulted in him becoming truly radioactive. The levels of radiation were so high coming off the victim, that the nurse treating him in the ambulance received a dangerous dose of radiation. That third victim expired in the ambulance within a few minutes. The ambulance was heavily contaminated. The roadways that the ambulance traveled became heavily contaminated and all three of the victims' remains had to be buried in lead caskets."

He continued and said, "I should tell you that in the SLI example, just a few pounds of radioactive material from the core produced thousands of tons of radioactive waste. The contamination caused by eight explosions in this case may easily reach that number. Especially if the contamination is spread along the roadways throughout the community and should tidal forces come into play along the contaminated sections of the beach."

He continued, "One final point if I may. Only three people were present at the site when the SL-1 reactor exploded and the vast majority of the radiation was contained within the reactor building, yet over 790 people received significant radiation exposures. The vast majority of these individuals were emergency responders and cleanup personnel."

Dr. Koskof looked around the table and said, "If these casts do contain radioactive material and are detonated, the long-term consequences of those detonations may be incalculable. This, ladies and gentlemen, may get very bad and stay bad for a very long time."

Chapter 24

A Night at the Beach

As Dr. Koskof was addressing all those gathered in the County Executive's conference room, Jack Ford was sitting in his Dodge pickup truck watching the waves crash into the shore of Asparagus Beach in Amagansett.

This was his third attempt at burying his little surprise package. He had driven here on the two previous nights but had been prevented from doing what needed to be done. The first night he was here the moon and stars were shining just a little too brightly for Jack Ford. He was convinced that he would be seen digging his hole. The second night was perfect as far as the weather was concerned. The night was overcast and there was a mist in the air. What had stopped him then was the young couple who arrived at the beach in their little Honda Accord right after he did. After an hour, they had still not gotten out of their car, and he decided to leave.

As he sat there watching the waves, he knew he was cutting it close timing-wise. The idiot government leaders would have probably received his letter today. He knew that it would be at least 24 to 48 hours before somebody had the bright idea to start patrolling the beaches.

This night turned out to be perfect. There was a light rain and the wind was blowing. Ford took one more look around the beach parking lot, assured himself that it was empty, and headed down the beach with shovel in hand. Ford chose a spot just east of the road and just below the high tide mark.

By the strangest coincidence, the spot Ford chose to hold his deadly device was within just a few yards of the very spot that Nazi saboteurs had buried their explosives over 75 years ago. Also, by the strangest of coincidences, the spot he chose sat in the shadow of the very sand dune used by an enraged

Son-of-Sam as he watched the frolicking young girls and planned their mass murder decades ago. Ford didn't know exactly why, but he really liked this spot. He took one quick look up and down the dark beach and then he started to dig.

Thirty minutes later, Ford was back at his pickup truck and had loaded the first part of his device on to his balloon-wheeled beach cart. He was proud of this first part of the bomb. It was the part that he had made. It was essentially an empty steel trash can lined with lots of explosives and all wired together with krytron switches.

Once the can was placed into the hole, he would then lower the concrete cast into the open center space of the steel can. He would then remove the concrete lid from the cast and put the light trash can lid in its place. He believed that with this bomb design the force of the blast would be directed upward and carry with it tiny little blown-up pieces of the isotope.

He returned to his pickup truck and rolled the concrete cast on his cart across the sand. He got to his newly dug hole and used a few well-placed ropes and poles to lower the heavy cast into his device. He reached down and set the bomb's timer for 2:00 pm the next day. He then straddled the hole and reached down and grasped the iron ring sunk into the lid of the concrete cast and pulled hard. Using all of his strength, he lifted the concrete lid to the edge of the hole and reached for the metal trash can cover. As he lifted the concrete lid off the cast, he caught a glimpse of some grey pieces of metal sitting at the bottom. He quickly slipped the metal trash can cover into place. His device was now sealed nice and tight, except for the high energy stream of gamma rays that were cutting through both the garbage can's steel lid and Jack Ford's body.

On the drive back to Hampton Bays it occurred to Ford that he had not given any thought at all as to how he was going to get his money. Clearly, wherever the money goes, he thought now, there will be an army of cops. Maybe even FBI agents. Then there were the tracking devices and helicopters. The thought of perhaps using Zabo to pick up the money popped into his head. As he passed over the Shinnecock Canal he decided not to think about the money just yet. He still had quite a lot to do. He planned on calling the County Executive's office and the press in the morning. He really did want the cops to have enough time to find and examine his device. That should put the fear of God into them. If they don't pay up after that, he thought, he will let one go off. Besides, he thought, "I have seven casts. That's seven big booms. They will pay me sooner or later."

Chapter 25

Operation Apollo Lives

The logistical capabilities of the Israeli Mossad had long been the envy of many intelligence agencies. Once a decision was made to proceed with an operation, all of the usual bureaucratic problems just seemed to vanish. People were moved quickly to where they had to be and any equipment needed for that particular operation was quickly obtained and pre-positioned.

For this unique operation the Mossad had chosen five experienced agents. One of those agents had been in the U.S. for over a year. He had been told to drop all other assignments and only focus on the issue involving the stolen Highly Enriched Uranium. He was also told that he would be leaving the country at the end of this assignment and would not be returning. The team of five agents needed a fishing boat capable of navigating in both the Atlantic and the shallow waters in and around Shinnecock Bay. They also needed several Ludlum Geiger counters and five Beretta 92FSR silenced pistols.

The person chosen to lead this operation was Josh Gallin. He had been a member of the Mossad's Special Operations Department for eight years. Prior to that he had served for 10 years within the Israeli Defense Force and had risen to the rank of Major.

Gallin had been fully briefed on the details of the original failed Operation Apollo from the 1960s. He had also been briefed on the disappearance and presumed death of Mossad agent Aharon Kagan in 1977. Kagan's mission had been to confirm the presence of the uranium inside a particular operative's building in Hampton Bays. He was supposed to be meeting a descendent of the Levy family to obtain that confirmation. It was later reported by embassy personnel that both Kagan and the Levy family descendent he was supposed to be meeting had disappeared. Gallin was also made aware of the tremendous political ramifications on the international front should the world become aware of Israel's past, and highly illegal, uranium procurement program.

Josh Gallin's mission was clear. Go to the building and seize the uranium. He was then to remove it by boat and transfer it to a waiting Israeli freighter 10 miles off the coast of Long Island.

Should the uranium not be in the barn, he was to find it.

Josh checked into a room at the Colonial Shores Hotel in a section of Hampton Bays known as Tiana. He and his team had arrived at JFK late the previous night and had been driven to a newly-purchased boat which was awaiting them at a small marina just south of the Shinnecock Canal. Before departing the marina, they were given two large Pelican Cases containing their requested equipment. They were also given the keys to their already-paid-for hotel rooms. The boat was driven by Josh from the marina to Tiana Bay and was now tied up at the end of the Colonial Shores dock. They were now only a 15-minute boat ride away from Smith Creek and the old barn.

Josh unpacked the few personal items he had with him and obtained a bottle of water from the small refrigerator in his room. He checked to ensure that all of the curtains in the room were closed. He then fired up his laptop and began downloading the latest reports that had been copied from the Joint Terrorism Task Force and Suffolk County Police servers, as well as some very interesting meeting notes that had been scanned into the County Executive's server at 2:00 am that morning.

Chapter 26

Jake's Dilemma

Jake had decided that he would brief Lieutenant Blair as soon as he got into the office. First, however, he wanted to talk to Patti Ball about the telephone conversation he had had with Zabo and about the photo that Zabo had emailed him. Wanna-be wise guys like Patti Ball never give up much unless their own ass is on the line. Since Jake didn't have anything on Ball at the moment, he doubted Ball would be cooperative. When he arrived at Ball's place of business he found that it was completely shut down. No trucks, no cars, no people, and all the lights were out in the little office building. It was clear he would have to come back later that day.

Jake left Patti Ball's place and headed for his office. Just as he was pulling into the police headquarters parking lot his cell phone rang. It was Sue Beacher from the M.E.s office.

"Hi, Sue. What's going on?"

Sue said, "I need to see you about your new friend Zabo. How soon can you get here?"

Jake asked, "Can it wait until this afternoon? I'm about to brief my boss on the case."

She said, "You're going to want to talk to me first. How soon?"

Jake said, "I'm leaving headquarters now. I'll see you in 20 minutes."

Twenty minutes later Jake walked into Sue Beacher's office. "Here I am," said Jake. "What's so urgent?"

Sue replied, "I got this at eight o'clock this morning." She handed Jake a copy of an email and attachment sent to all M.E.'s office personnel by the M.E himself. The subject line simply said "urgent – see attached."

Jake looked at the attachment and saw immediately that it was an alert from the JTTF in New York City. The notice stated that they were looking for information regarding any cases involving recent exposure to radiation. There was a contact name and number at the bottom of the page. Jake made a note of the information.

"Jake, do you know what this is about?" Sue asked.

Jake looked up from the document and said, "No, not a clue, and it might not be related to my case at all."

Sue smiled and said sarcastically, "Fat chance they're not related. You know I have to report the Zabo Pruit results and I have to report it now. I just wanted to give you a heads up."

"Okay," said Jake. "Do what you have to do. If you hear anything else, please call me right away."

Jake left the building and headed for John Flynn's office next door at the D.A.'s office. When he entered John's office he found him on the phone. John pointed at the coffee pot and Jake went over to help himself. John hung up the phone and said, "If you haven't briefed your boss yet, you better get your ass moving. There's something big going on. E.S. just called and wanted to know how many Geiger counters and radiation pagers we had in our inventory and how many trained people we had to operate them. Like I said, something big is going on." John leaned forward and asked, "Care to fill me in?"

Jake said, "I really don't know." He proceeded to tell John about this morning's conversation with Sue Beacher.

When he was done, John reached into his desk drawer and pulled out a black device about the size of a deck of cards. "Here," he said. "Turn this switch on. Keep it on. The batteries are good for days. Hang it on your belt. If it makes a noise, run the other way and call E.S."

On that cheery note Jake said goodbye to his friend and headed to his car. It was time to see his boss.

In the homicide squad room Jake saw half a dozen detectives working at their desks. One of them was Holly Gilpin. She was busy on a call but looked up and waved as he passed her. Jake went straight to his Lieutenant's office and found him sitting at his little conference table. Jillian was nowhere to be seen.

Jake said, "Hey, Lieutenant. Got a minute? I want to bring you up-to-date on the Zabo Pruit case."

Blair looked at Jake with a look of complete puzzlement on his face.

Jake said, "The body in the car. In Hampton Bays. You gave me the case because it was close to home."

"Oh, yeah," said Blair. "Now I remember. How is the case going?"

With that, Jake told the Lieutenant everything he had done on the case to date. Well, almost everything. Jake had been debating the Betsy Vail issue in his head all morning. He kept asking himself what should he do about the Betsy information. It was a simple lead that could mean nothing or it could mean everything. He decided to hold back on the Betsy lead until he had a chance to do some neighborhood interviews. Besides, that case was a long time ago and may not have been related at all.

Blair wasn't too excited about the JTTF alert sent to the M.E.s office. But he did want to know if Jake was planning on filling them in on his case at some point. Jake told Blair that he would be reaching out to them today. That seemed to make the Lieutenant happy. Jake thanked him for his time and left the Lieutenant's office just as Jillian Stark was coming in. She had a bag of sandwiches in her hand and noisily dropped them onto the little conference table. She reached for the door and closed it with a bit of a bang just as Jake had passed through. As it was being closed he heard her say to Blair, "What the hell did he want?"

Jake stopped at the office coffee pot and then went back to his desk. He picked up his desk phone and called the JTTF contact number listed at the bottom of the alert notice.

"This should be interesting," he thought to himself.

The man on the other end of the line politely told Jake that there was no one available to take his call at the moment, but took down Jake's contact information and said someone from the task force would get back to him today.

Jake hung up his phone and pushed back in his chair.

"All right," he said to himself. "The boss has been briefed, JTTF called…ass covered. Time to find out who or what killed Zabo Pruit."

Jake picked up his notebook, phone and coffee and headed for the squad room door. He didn't quite make it. He heard the Lieutenant call his name and since he wasn't out the door yet, he had to turn around. "Yes, Lieutenant?" answered Jake.

"Could we see you for a moment?" asked the Lieutenant.

Jake could see Jillian standing behind the Lieutenant. He could also see that his Lieutenant was still holding his sandwich in his hand. Both he and Jillian were standing next to Jillian's desk. Jake walked over to them. The Lieutenant said, "Jake, we have some concerns regarding how you have handled the Pruit case and…"

Jillian interrupted and said in a very loud voice, "You have put the Lieutenant and the department in a very bad position!"

Jake, his eyes never leaving the Lieutenant, said, "Perhaps we should discuss this in your office, Sir."

"No," interrupted Jillian again. "The squad should hear this. You did not keep me informed as to what was going on in your case and now the JTTF is involved."

Jake, still not looking at Jillian, said, "I left your office less than 10 minutes ago and there were no issues. Why is there an issue now?"

"Well…" said the Lieutenant. "…the brass upstairs might see it as…"

Jillian jumped in again and this time shouted, "They might see it as you are an asshole and fuckup, Tucker!"

Jake turned towards Jillian. He put his phone and notebook down on her desk. As he went to put down his coffee cup it tipped over. All ten ounces went spilling across her desk, soaking everything in its path.

The look on Jillian's face was a combination of pure hatred and total bewilderment. "You did that on purpose!" she shouted. "How am I supposed to work now in this pile of filth?"

The Lieutenant, his eyes scanning the squad room, said, "Jillian, you need to calm down..."

"Don't tell me to calm down, look at what he did. How am I ever going to get that clean?" Jillian reached into the lower drawers of her desk and began pulling out cleaning supplies, a box of dust masks and a large pair of yellow rubber gloves. They were the long kind that went all the way to the elbow. In a rage Jillian tossed files and notebooks onto the floor and started putting on her mask and gloves.

Jake saw the Lieutenant slowly backing up towards his office. Still numb from what was happening right in front of him, Jake turned to look around the squad room. Every person in the room, except Detective Holly Gilpin, was standing and staring at the bizarre scene unfolding in front of them.

Holly, with a smile on her face and a cell phone in hand, was filming the entire show.

Jake picked up his soaked notebook and phone and headed for the door.

Jake went straight to Patti Ball's place of business. He was hoping that Ball would at least tell him where Zabo was staying. Based on Zabo's physical condition right before he died, it was clear to Jake that Zabo had been staying somewhere in Hampton Bays. Since Jeannine Pruit said Zabo was staying with his friend Ford, a lead on who Ford was would be very helpful right about now. He had already requested the cell phone tower ping data from Zabo's phone and he fully expected that to corroborate his theory.

Jake pulled his car right in front of the little office and got out. There was now a Jeep parked on the side of the building but nothing else seemed to have changed since his previous visit that morning. Jake climbed the cement block steps, knocked loudly on the door and stepped aside. He listened for any sound of movement from inside the office, then looked up and looked across the yard for any signs of movement. He knocked on the door again and this time he shouted, “Mr. Ball, it’s the Suffolk County Police! I need to speak with you for a minute!”

There was still no sound of movement. Jake thought it might be best to come back in the evening or perhaps just after sunrise.

He decided to check out the Jeep and get a photo of the license plate. When he walked up to the Jeep, he rested his left hand on the hood. “Still warm,” he thought. He noted that the driver’s side window was broken as if someone had broken into the Jeep. He bent his knees so that he could look directly through the hole in the glass.

“Oh shit,” he said out loud, and dropped to the ground and drew his Glock.

He started his scan with his weapon pointed out in front of him. His front gunsight followed his eyes as they moved from left to right and then right to left. He had a choice to make now. Use his cell phone or get to the police radio in his car. Help would come much faster if he used the radio.

Jake sprinted for his car. He reached in with his right foot and pressed down on the brake and then he hit the ignition button. His eyes were constantly scanning the area surrounding him. His police radio lit up and he reached for the handset and keyed the microphone. “Ninety-nine Frank to headquarters,” he said to the dispatcher.

“Ninety-nine Frank standby,” the dispatcher said.

“Ninety-nine Frank to headquarters emergency traffic.”

“Go ahead.”

“Requesting immediate backup to 198 B-like-boy North Street, Manorville. I have a male subject down with multiple gunshot wounds. Approach with caution, shooter may be active.”

Jake dropped the microphone onto the seat of his car, put both hands on his Glock and scanned again. A minute or two later, off in the distance, he heard the sound of a siren.

By the time dusk fell Jake had been sitting in his car for over an hour. Emergency Service Units had swept the office and small outbuildings. They found no sign of anyone else being present or hiding on the grounds. The Lieutenant had sent Holly Gilpin to handle the investigation. Jake had found the body, which made him a witness in the case, so someone else would need to take the lead.

His passenger door opened and Holly slid into the passenger seat. "You good?" she asked.

"Yeah I'm good. But it's been a helluva day."

"Why were you here, Jake?"

"I was looking for Patti Ball. He's the owner of this place. My recent corpse called and emailed Ball the day he died. I had questions for him but he wasn't here."

Holly said, "Oh, he was here all right. He was probably not feeling up to answering any of your questions with those three bullets in his head. Make that two bullets. Looks like one of them went straight through. Big caliber, big holes, big mess."

She continued, "Your corpse. Is that the case the wicked witch of the east was screaming about in the squad room today?"

Jake nodded and said, "Yeah, that's the one. The case has hair all over it. Can I fill you in in the morning? It's a long story and I'm exhausted."

"No problem," said Holly. "Go, get some sleep."

As she was getting out of his car she said, "Oh, by the way. You might want to check out a video someone posted on YouTube today. It's titled 'Female Cop Goes Wild.' Fun stuff. Check it out."

Jake had just gotten to the end of Ponquogue Avenue in Hampton Bays. He was now sitting at the stop sign and had closed both of his eyes. If he made a left, he would be at his home on Lighthouse Road in five minutes. If he turned right, he could do a quick drive-by of Betsy Vail's old residence on Oak Lane. He opened his eyes, sighed, and put his right turn blinker on.

Jake's drive-by of the house at 14 Oak Lane didn't provide him with much information. There was a porch light on, but no cars in the driveway. He drove to the end of Oak Lane and stopped his car. He had a really nice view of Smith Creek directly in front of him. The stars were shining off the water and there was still a thin orange line running right across the western horizon. The striped bass were jumping all over the place, being chased by a school of bluefish. He could see a fishing boat moving slowly through the creek.

Jake thought to himself, "This is why I live in this town." He then turned his car around and headed back towards number 14.

Jake made the same left-hand turn he had made the other day. It was the first left turn after number 14. This time, Jake happened to glance at the green and white street sign on the corner. One of the signs said Oak Lane. The other sign, which was for the street Jake was now driving on, said Mill Race Road. Jake drove another 50 feet before he stopped his car in the middle of the street.

"Mill Race? Mill Race?" Jake repeated to himself. Then he slapped the steering wheel and said out loud, "Got it."

He swung his car around and headed home.

Close to 11 pm, Jake was still working at his computer. The stack of empty K-cups next to the coffee machine in his kitchen was evidence of the numerous times he had refilled his coffee cup. When he had gotten home, he had begun to check all of the county property records for the people living on Mill Race Road.

The scrap of paper he had removed from Zabo's car at the police impound yard had led Jake to this point. Zabo must have been staying with Ford on Mill Race Road. Now he had to find Ford. Assuming that Ford was Zabo's friend's last name, and assuming he owned a home on the street, it would show up in the county deed records. If this didn't work, he had plans to get out early in the morning and collect every license plate number on the block.

His plans for the next morning reminded him that he had already photographed a few plate numbers on the street during his first visit to Betsy Vail's old house. Jake got up from his desk to find his cell phone. As he was passing through the kitchen there was a knock at his side door.

Jake was surprised by the sound not just because of the lateness of the hour but also because no one had knocked on his door for over a year. He instinctively reached for his Glock, which was sitting on top of his cell phone on the kitchen counter.

Glock in hand, he opened the door a few inches.

The man on the porch said, "Detective Tucker, I'm Special Agent Bob Morse from the JTTF. You called my office this morning."

Morse had his credentials in his hand. Jake saw the familiar large letters of the FBI stamped onto the ID card.

Jake opened the door further and gestured for him to come in. Jake pointed to his small kitchen table and said, "Please, take a seat here." When Morse sat, Jake asked, "Coffee?"

"No, thanks," said Morse. "I tried to call your cell several times today. There was no answer. Also, your voice mailbox is full so I couldn't leave a message."

Jake said, "That's odd. I didn't get any calls this afternoon." He picked up his phone off the table and turned it over to look at the screen. The screen was dark. He hit the power button and nothing happened. He said, "I don't get it. It had a full charge this morning."

As he was about to put the phone back down on the table, he saw a tiny drop of brown liquid fall from the phone. "Uh oh," Jake said. "Somebody spilled a cup of coffee on it this morning. That could be the problem. I'll try and get it fixed tomorrow."

Morse nodded and said, "What can you tell me about the death of Zabo Pruit?"

Jake replied, "Well, you obviously have already spoken to Sue Beacher. Most of what I know comes from her report. I am still tracking down leads. Can you give me some general idea as to what this is about?"

Morse replied, "I can't. The only thing I can say is that it is an ongoing FBI investigation. Can you tell me about the leads you are following?"

Jake stared into Morse's eyes and said, "I can't. The only thing I can say is that it is an ongoing Suffolk County Police homicide investigation."

Morse, unfazed by Jake's sarcastic answer, asked, "Can you tell me about Patrick Ball?"

Jake replied, "Sure. He's dead."

Morse asked, "Can you tell me a little more than that?"

Jake replied, "Sure, he's very dead. But in order to shorten this one-sided conversation I will tell you that he died before I could speak to him."

Morse asked, "Can you tell me why you wanted to speak to him?"

Jake replied, "I can't. The only thing I can say is that it is an ongoing Suffolk County Police homicide investigation."

Jake and Morse stared at each other from across the table for a full minute before Morse said, "Okay, we will have do this another way."

Jake responded, "Probably not."

Morse stood up.

Jake said, "Well, you have been an absolute delight and the top-off for a truly wonderful day. Let me show you the way out."

Chapter 27

Hole in the Sand

As Jake slept at his computer in his dining room, George Philips and his three friends had just met each other at the Exit 66 Park & Ride on the eastern end of the Long Island Expressway. George was a 70-year-old Vietnam veteran, a chopper pilot who had flown Hueys in and out of Cambodia during the war. He had later become a successful Certified Public Accountant thanks to Uncle Sam's GI Bill.

He and his three friends were all retired gentlemen who belonged to the Atlantic Treasure Club. The Club was Long Island's oldest metal detecting club. These four members liked to get together one day a month and search for lost treasures on the numerous beaches along the Atlantic coast of Long Island.

George Philips had been a member of the Club for over twenty-five years and had searched for treasures from Rockaway Beach all the way to Montauk Point. During this time, he had discovered a total of two hundred and thirty-seven dollars in change, four watches, six religious medals, seventeen steel-cased bullets of various calibers, and the body of a drowned surfer that had been brought in by the incoming tide.

Today was the group's treasure hunting day and they were heading to a stretch of beach at the end of Atlantic Avenue in Amagansett. They had to be there by dawn in order to finish their sweeps before the beach crowds arrived. According to the Club's records, the locals called that particular stretch of sand Asparagus Beach and it supposedly catered to the very rich and famous. That made it the perfect place for George and his little circle of friends to search for lost treasures.

It was close to 9:00 am. George and his friends had formed a skirmish line and had surveyed most of Asparagus Beach over the last two hours. They were now moving east to west along the high tide mark. This was going to be their last run-through before they packed up and went to breakfast.

George knew that whatever his device had just detected was big. He had gotten readings like this before and it was usually an old iron anchor or a part to a car that had long ago been abandoned on the beach.

His fellow treasure hunters all stopped and watched as George fell to his knees and began to dig in the sand. After about three minutes of digging his hand scraped against something metallic. A little more digging revealed a handle attached to some kind of metal cover.

George reached into the hole, grabbed the exposed handle and pulled. He lifted what looked like a galvanized steel trash can cover over his head and shouted, "I've been looking for one of these!"

Everyone laughed as George stood up.

Then George looked down into the hole and froze.

It was close to 9:00 am and Jack Ford was driving his pickup truck north on Flanders Road. He was heading towards the town of Riverhead which was the actual County Seat. Although all of the powerful and important people in the county government pretty much stayed on the western end of the county, he felt that making the call from the County Seat parking lot added a little to the "in your face thing." He also thought that it might be wise to have his throw-away cell phone ping off of a tower outside of Hampton Bays. He wasn't absolutely sure what the cops could do or not do with tracing cell phone calls these days, but he knew he didn't want to take any chances.

Ten minutes later Ford pulled his pickup truck into the county center's parking lot. He picked a spot on the far western side near the center's power plant. He took a folded piece of paper from his pocket and spread it out on the seat next to him. There were two phone numbers written in big block print on the paper. One was for the County

Executive's office. The other was for News12, Long Island's main television station.

The Easthampton Township Police's jurisdiction included the tiny hamlet of Amagansett. It was this agency that received George Philip's initial 911 call.

Easthampton Patrolman Bruce Spears had been on the job for eight years. He was one of those cops whose everyday goal was to get home in one piece at the end of the day. He had a wife and four young children and he knew he had to act cautiously and professionally every time he stepped out in public wearing his uniform.

In response to the information given in the 911 call, Spears was now walking on Asparagus Beach just two paces behind George Philips. Just ahead of them, Spears could see a metal trash can cover and a small pile of sand. George Philips stopped at the edge of the pile of sand and pointed downwards. Officer Spears looked at the hole in the sand where Philips was pointing. He then leaned slightly forward and saw what looked like some sort of timing device, wires and possibly explosives sitting inside of a metal trash can.

Spears pulled his head and shoulders back immediately.

He turned to Philips and yelled, "Run, now!"

Philips took off at a sprint. Spears was right behind him.

The total radiation exposure time for Patrolman Spears was only a matter of seconds. Although there was some cell damage, Spears' body would heal itself over time.

George Philips wasn't as lucky. He had stood in the direct path of the Cobalt-60's gamma rays for close to four minutes. His ARS symptoms would begin within a few days. He would be dead in two weeks.

News12 Long Island was located in a town called Woodbury, just west of Suffolk County and about 75 miles west of Amagansett. The news station was quite efficient at fielding their mobile news units at disaster scenes, major crime scenes and other large newsworthy events. The producer on duty that day was trying desperately to decide if the call she had just hung up from was a crank call or a big story.

She kept glancing at the white-faced clock on the wall of the newsroom. The caller said the bomb would go off on Asparagus Beach in Amagansett at 2:00 pm and that there would be a lot of radiation. The producer knew that the station would need a least a half hour to get a crew and the satellite truck ready to go. Then there was the 2-hour-plus drive to Amagansett. She now had three people working the phones trying to confirm any part of what the caller had to say.

About 10 minutes later one of the staffers ran into the office and said, "We were just listening to the Suffolk Police scanner. They just dispatched their bomb trailer and techs to a beach in Easthampton."

The supervisor dialed the satellite truck bay.

"Get one ready to roll," she told them. "I want us on the road in 15 minutes."

The conference room in the County Executive's office was filled to capacity. The call had come in less than an hour ago. The caller had warned that an explosive device had been buried somewhere on or near Asparagus Beach in Amagansett and that the device contained radioactive material. The caller made no demands. He simply instructed them to find it before it exploded at 2:00 pm.

The County Executive looked around the room. They were rapidly losing control of the situation. Even the simplest task of arranging a video link with the Easthampton Town Supervisor and Police Chief had failed.

The FBI representative in the room kept trying to assure everyone that they could handle every aspect of this crisis and that their highly-vaunted Hazardous Material Response Unit was on their way from Quantico, Virginia. A public relations team from Brookhaven National Laboratory was also present and tried to assure everyone in the room that radiation was truly our friend and, despite what their colleague had told the County Executive the previous night, any radiation release would probably not be all that dangerous.

Unbeknownst to the County Executive, the emergency operations taking place in and around the beaches in Amagansett was in direct contrast as to what was happening at the seat of the county government. The Easthampton Police Department had been informed within the hour by first arriving Emergency Services units that the explosive device buried on their beach might contain radioactive material. Once the current and expected wind direction was determined, the police department had established a command post on the corner of Montauk Highway and Atlantic Avenue. All residents south of Montauk Highway to the shoreline were already being evacuated.

Emergency evacuation centers were being established at the elementary school, middle school and high school. Neighboring Southampton Town was preparing their emergency shelters to handle any overflow from Amagansett. Additional patrol units were being brought in from Southampton Township, and the State Police and beach patrol units had cleared the shoreline for 3 miles in each direction. The command post had requested and received helicopter surveillance support from both the Coast Guard and the Suffolk Police. Thanks to the singular efforts of Easthampton Town Patrolman Bruce Spears, not a single person had come within 300 yards of the explosive device since he secured the area as a crime scene.

Hazardous Materials Specialists from the County Police Emergency Service Unit arrived and began planning a mission to obtain radiation readings from the beach area. At 11:05 am, a heavily armored SWAT vehicle made its way down Atlantic Avenue. A Geiger counter probe had been attached to the roof of the vehicle and was being monitored continuously by a HazMat technician in the passenger seat.

By the time they reached the beach parking lot they had still not obtained any radiation readings.

The SWAT vehicle operator maneuvered the vehicle slowly onto the beach. Just as they passed the first sand dune the HazMat technician yelled, “Stop, back up!”

The needle on his Geiger counter had risen from “0” to “25 Roentgens” in the space of two seconds as they entered the beach. Now that they were behind the 6 tons of sand that made up the first dune, the Geiger counter had dropped back down to “0.”

The two bomb technicians in the back of the SWAT vehicle opened the rear doors and extended a ramp. Two minutes later a small tracked vehicle, operated by a remote and equipped with a Geiger counter, came down the ramp and headed for the beach. The robot’s job was to tell them how much radiation was present at the source and, via the video feed, tell them what kind of explosive device was present.

The little tracked vehicle trundled across the beach, headed for the little hole in the sand less than a hundred yards away.

Chapter 28

Beginning of a Long Day

Jake arrived at his office a few minutes after 9:00 am. He had a few things he needed to do before he could focus again on his Mill Race Road lead. He considered his first order of business to avoid another confrontation with his Lieutenant and his girlfriend. To his relief, the Lieutenant's office was dark and Jillian's sparking clean desk was completely devoid of any reports or papers. Jake took it as a good sign that she had not appeared in the squad room yet.

Jack slipped into his chair and dialed the technical support section. He desperately needed to get his phone working so he could access the license plate photos he had recorded on Mill Race Road. After ten rings someone in the technical support section finally answered the phone. Jake described the incident with the coffee and wanted to know if there was any way to retrieve the photo images on his phone.

The technician wanted assurance from Jake that, one, the images were not pornographic and, two, the phone had been drenched in coffee and not urine. It seemed that the major cause of death for department-issued cell phones was death by drowning in a porcelain bowl.

Jake assured him that the photos were potential evidence and that his phone now smelled like a rich Italian dark roast and not urine. The technician told him that he would take a look at Jake's phone and attempt to download Jake's image files from the cloud backup. He said he would email the images to Jake later that day. He also said that it would take a couple of days to get a new cell phone to Jake if his old one was dead.

Jake thanked the man and hung up. As he reached for his notebook, he thought to himself, "What the hell is a cloud backup?"

An hour later Detective Holly Gilpin walked into the squad room and sat down next to Jake at his desk. He expected her to start asking him about Patti Ball.

She surprised him by starting with, "Did you see the YouTube video I told you about?"

"No," said Jake. "I had a late-night visitor in the form of an FBI agent questioning me about Patti Ball."

She raised her eyebrows and asked, "Surprise, surprise. How did that go?"

He replied, "Not bad. We lied and patronized each other for a while. Then we went out for drinks and dancing. All in all, it was a nice evening."

Holly glanced over at the Lieutenant's office and said, "They both got calls from Internal Affairs late last night. It seems someone told the brass about the YouTube video. Both of them are in Internal Affairs right now giving statements. If all goes well, they may not be back."

Jake said, "Wow, all this over a spilled cup of coffee."

Holly replied, "Speaking of that, there is an office pool going on. Bets are being made as to whether you spilled that coffee on purpose or not. I've got five bucks riding on the theory that you knew about her little proclivity towards cleanliness all along."

Jake smiled and said, "If I did, I would never tell. After all, everyone knows that I am the epitome of discretion."

Both Holly and Jake had a good laugh over that line.

Finally, Holly said, "Now tell me all about Patti Ball and how he fits into your fried corpse case."

Jake started talking and kept talking for over 30 minutes. He then showed Holly Zabo's cell phone. He brought up both the email and attached photograph sent to Ball the day Zabo died.

Just as he was finishing, one of the day shift homicide detectives came into the squad room and said, "Hey, you should turn on News12. Something's going on out in Easthampton. E.S. is there."

It was now a little after one o'clock in the afternoon. The Easthampton Town Police were having a difficult time keeping Montauk Highway open. The eastbound lane of Montauk Highway was jammed with emergency vehicles and media satellite trucks. The westbound lane was jammed with fleeing vacationers and residents who just wanted to get out of town.

News12 had announced the detonation time and the fact that there might be a radiation release. This news produced a mass exodus and traffic gridlock that stretched for 27 miles.

It was decision time for the E.S. commander. In the last hour, several different plans had been examined in an effort to render the explosive device safe. One plan involved removing the concrete cast to a safe distance, using remotes to remove the radioactive material and then setting a charge to blow up the remaining explosive. The problem was the cast itself. There was no place for the robot to grasp the cast and even if it could, the robot's arm was not designed to support that much weight. Every other plan involved bomb technicians having extended contact with the device and potentially receiving a lethal dosage of radiation. It was finally decided that an attempt would be made to disrupt the device with a high-powered water cannon.

By 1:43 pm the robot operator, locked down inside the armored SWAT vehicle, had maneuvered the robot to the edge of the hole. He manipulated the robot's arm to point downward. The video camera on the robot's arm was now serving two functions. First, it was acting as a gun sight with its crosshairs settled on what the bomb technicians believed to be the key electronic components of the bomb's detonator. Next, the robot arm was serving as a platform for a water cannon nozzle attached to its grappler. A high-pressure water supply had been established through several hundred feet of fire hose and a hydrant located in the beach parking lot.

The robot operator keyed his portable radio and said, “Ready.”

There were three blasts from an air horn that could be heard for a half a mile.

Then the robot operator keyed his radio again and said, in a calm voice, “Fire in the hole.”

He toggled a small switch on his remote-control panel. The tiny light above the switch turned green.

A large “CRACK” was heard up and down the beach as thousands of pounds of water pressure disintegrated the bomb’s electronic components.

The E.S. commander and the Easthampton Police Chief both watched the disruption of the device on a live video feed inside the command post. The image displayed on the large TV screen clearly showed that the water cannon charge had done its intended work.

The E.S. commander looked at his watch and saw that it was 1:50 pm.

He turned to the Police chief and said, “Now comes the hard part.”

Chapter 29

Working Without a Net

It was now mid-afternoon and Jake was following the events in Amagansett closely. He had no idea if Agent Morse had attempted to reach him again on his cell. However, he suspected that if Morse really needed to talk to him, he would call his office phone. Jake also suspected that Morse would be knee-deep in whatever was happening in Amagansett.

Jake wanted to get back into the field to try and locate Ford but was concerned that he would miss a call from Morse. Finally he recorded a short message on his office phone telling callers to contact the command frequency dispatcher should they need to reach him immediately. Jake then made a quick call to his technical support section. He let the phone ring twenty times. No one answered. Frustrated, Jake pushed back in his chair and thought about how odd it felt to not have a working cell phone right next to him. It had become an important part of his professional life and he had never realized how much he relied upon it. He felt like he was working without a net.

The news about what was happening in Amagansett had gone viral and now every major network provided a steady stream of experts who were long on opinions but apparently short on practical experience. The public was getting what they believed to be news from a long series of talking heads all jostling with each other for air time.

The talking heads appeared to have their biggest impact upon the rich and famous who were vacationing in the summer mansions in Easthampton. This group of people was also affectionately known as the "big donor class."

Ford was wrong about these individuals reaching out to local government officials with concerns about their personal financial losses. Many of these individuals bypassed local politicians completely and made their calls directly to the

Governor's private cell phone number. Some even reached out to senior staff members at the White House.

Things on the ground were not much better when it came to the media. Numerous individuals had been apprehended trying to sneak through the evacuation zone. All were members of the media.

The worst incident occurred as a pair of robots was attempting to lay lead-lined blankets over the top of the concrete cast. Even though a 5-mile "no fly" zone had been established around the bomb site, a helicopter loaded with media people swooped in and hoovered 15 feet above the working robots. The resulting sandstorm from the rotor wash was enough to damage both robots' video camera lenses. After hovering over the site for more than two minutes, the helicopter took off in a southerly direction, chased by a Coast Guard HH-65 Dolphin copter. The crew of the Coast Guard copter managed to get the tail number of the pursued aircraft. It took FAA criminal investigators three days to track down the pilot and his three media passengers. Each was informed that they had, in all likelihood, received a lethal dose of radiation.

Jake went to his car and headed for Hampton Bays. He was planning on driving up and down Mill Race Road and recording as many vehicle plate numbers as he could. Since his cell phone was dead, he would have to do it the old-fashioned way and just write them down. He planned to use the computer at his house to run each of the plates. If no leads popped up, he would do another drive-through and look for additional plates.

As Jake headed eastbound on the Sunrise Highway, he never noticed the late model sedan following him at a distance. It was the same make and model driven by the FBI.

Chapter 30

The Road to Perdition Ends at a Barn

It was early evening and Jake was sitting at the computer in his dining room. He had made one drive-through down Mill Race Road late that afternoon and had managed to pick up four plate numbers. He had run all four through the Department of Motor Vehicles computer portal and none had come back with the owner's name being Ford.

Jake decided to turn on the TV and check for an update as to what was happening on the beach in Amagansett. Every news channel seemed to have a panel of experts espousing various doomsday opinions as to the consequences of a radiation release on the white sands of the Hamptons. One station featured an historian who spoke about Nazi saboteurs and the serial killer Son-of-Sam, who all seemed to have occupied that very same stretch of beach at some point in the past. Finally, he came across a newscaster who was reporting from the front of one of the emergency evacuation shelters in Easthampton and was actually relaying news.

As Jake raised the volume, he heard the newscaster say, "...and using a remote-controlled boom type device were able to then lower a concrete slab over what they have been referring to as a cast. It is this opened cast that is believed to contain the highly radioactive material. According to a source who was present at the site, and I am quoting him now, 'it was like turning off a light switch the moment the cover was in place.'"

"Prior to that," the newscaster continued, "as we reported earlier today, robots were used to remove the explosives surrounding the buried cast. Then lead-lined blankets from Brookhaven National Laboratory were flown by helicopter to what is called the staging area about two miles east of where we are now. They were transported by truck to the beach. Using robots again, the blankets were placed over the sunken device, acting as a temporary shield so workers could widen the top of the hole, in order to accommodate the concrete slab cover we just told you about. The authorities reportedly wanted to get all the loose sand out of the way to ensure a tight seal once the lid was in place."

"Now, here is the real interesting part of this story. The lead blankets did not eliminate all of the radiation emitting from the bomb, they only reduced it. The radiation levels were still extremely high. So the emergency workers, who all volunteered for this, by the way, were only allowed to work around the now-diffused bomb for a very short time. We later found out that the very short time was defined in seconds. They were actually timed with a stopwatch and an air horn would sound when they had to leave. They were not allowed to go back in again and had to leave the site. It reportedly took five two-person teams of volunteers just to remove a few pounds of loose sand from around the opening in the ground."

"Our last report from the site was that the radiation is, in fact, now contained and several emergency workers are now clearing and widening the area around the device, and a small pay loader is being used to build some type of downward-sloping ramp."

The news station then went to a commercial break and Jake went back to his computer.

Jake pushed back from his desk, checked his watch and saw that it was a little after 9:00 pm. He realized he had not eaten anything since that morning and decided to make himself a sandwich. As he entered his kitchen, he heard his house phone ring. He went back to his desk and picked up the receiver.

He said, "Tucker,"

A male voice said, "Detective, this is Max from the Tech Section at headquarters. The day man left me a note about your phone. I've downloaded your pictures from the Cloud as you requested and I emailed them to your office email account. Do you have remote access to your email account?"

Jake replied, "Yes, I do, thanks." He continued, "By the way, what about my voicemails and text messages from today?"

"Uh, hold on." There was a short pause and then Max returned and said, "I just double-checked. There weren't any."

Jake thanked Max and hung up the phone. "That's odd," he thought to himself. "You would think someone from the task force would be reaching out for me. Last night they were banging down my front door. Today, the shit hits the fan and then nothing."

Jake forgot all about his sandwich and quickly opened the email containing his cell phone photos. There were several shots of Betsy Vail's old house taken from various street angles. There were also eighteen photos for the six license plate numbers he had previously collected on Mill Race Road. He had taken a photo of each license plate, then had zoomed out so he could identify the vehicle's make and model. He then zoomed out even further so that he could see which vehicle was parked in front of each house. Close up, mid-range and overall shots. Just like they taught him at detective school.

Jake noted that he had already picked up two of the plate numbers in the photos he took today. That left four plates to run through the Department of Motor Vehicle portal. Jake had completed running three of the plates when his telephone rang again. He quickly glanced at his watch and saw that it was well after 10:00 pm.

He lifted the receiver and said, "Tucker."

"Jake, it's me, Holly. I just wanted to tell you that I took a run at Zabo's wife Jeannine this evening. Since Zabo was one of the last people that we know about to call Ball, I figured she might remember something else. She was pretty drunk when I talked to her and we had a hard time communicating. The only thing she told me, that she didn't tell you, was that she looked up Ball's number for Zabo in Zabo's old address book. I got the book. I thought there might be a lead in there for you. I know you're trying to find out who he was staying with. I'm working nights tonight. Want me to drop the book off?"

Jake replied, "Good news. I have been running into nothing but dead ends. No, no need to come way out east tonight." Jake paused and then said, "You know, you could thumb through the pages and see if you can find any reference to a guy named Ford, first or last, or a street named Mill Race."

He added, "I may have to go out for a little while and you know my cell is dead. If you find anything, just leave me a message on my house phone." He thanked Holly again for her call and then hung up the phone.

His attention shifted back to his computer screen. All of a sudden he wasn't quite sure what he was looking at. Then he remembered that just before the phone rang, he had entered the last of the license plate numbers from his cell phone photos. There, right in front him on the screen, was the name Jack Ford. It was the registration information from the license plate belonging to a black late model Dodge pickup truck. The registration said that Ford lived on Highview Drive in the Town of Babylon, which was over 50 miles away from the shore of Shinnecock Bay where Zabo died.

Jake searched for a driver's license and came up with a photo of Ford. The driver's license had the same Babylon home address as the registration. He then looked at the overall photo showing where the Dodge pickup was parked. It was in a driveway on Mill Race just a short distance from Betsy's old home on Oak Lane. Jake dug through his reams of printouts, looking for the County's property map that showed each parcel on the block and the current owner's name.

He finally found the map he was looking for and compared it to the photos he had taken with his cell phone.

The black Dodge pickup was parked in the driveway that belonged to 106 Mill Race Road. The property map showed that the eastern edge of the property bordered on the backyard of Betsy's old home. Jake looked at the owner's name for 106. The property belonged to a Mrs. Wilma Babcock with an address in Jacksonville, Florida.

"A rental," Jake thought. He jumped up from his desk and headed for the kitchen. He grabbed his keys and his Glock and headed for the door. He stopped for a second and looked around his kitchen for his cell phone and then remembered where it was. He then went out the door and got into his car.

Just down the street from Jake's house was a little seafood market. The name on the sign at the top of the building said "Tully's" and it had a reputation for having the best seafood in town. The market had been closed for several hours and its parking lot, bordering on Lighthouse Road, sat in complete darkness. As Jake left his driveway and headed north, he didn't notice a late model sedan sitting in the parking lot of Tully's. Just as Jake passed, the lone occupant of the vehicle turned on the headlights and pulled the sedan onto Lighthouse Road.

...

As Jake was approaching Mill Race Road, four men were aboard a fishing boat that had just passed Tiana's East Point and turned north to enter Smith Creek. Piloting the boat was Agent Josh Gallin of the Israeli Mossad. He and his three companions had emptied their rooms at the Colonial Shores Hotel. They had removed their personal belongings, equipment and every scrap of trash. They were well aware that every empty coffee cup and every used piece of discarded dental floss was a potential prison sentence. Each man had also painstakingly wiped down every surface within each room to remove any trace of them ever having been there.

Gallin looked at his watch; it was now close to midnight. He thought that with any luck, he and his team would be heading for home aboard an Israeli freighter in just under two hours.

...

Jake decided to enter the Mill Race Road neighborhood from a different direction. This time he made a left on Nautilus Drive and took it straight south to the shore of the bay where it connected to the end of Oak Lane. He grabbed his flashlight and stepped out of his car. He looked up to see some breaks in the clouds, revealing a few dimly lit stars and a hazy moon. He looked out over the bay and could just make out Tiana's East Point over a half mile away. He saw a late-night fisherman gliding his boat through the calm water heading into Smith Creek. He turned his back to the water and started walking down Oak Lane.

...

Jack Ford had just climbed up his basement stairs and laid the box he was carrying down on his kitchen table. He checked the clock on the wall and saw that it was a few minutes after midnight. After he had made his calls from Riverhead, he had stopped at several different stores to pick up a few needed sundries like wire, solder and 9-volt batteries. He then stopped for lunch at a little restaurant on East Main Street in Riverhead called the Rendezvous.

From there he headed to a bar on the west end of Hampton Bays called the Boardy Barn. He liked the Boardy Barn. It was quiet in there in the daytime and no matter which way you turned your head you would see a TV hanging from the ceiling or one bolted to a wall.

He spent his afternoon there sipping beer after beer and gleefully enjoying the events that were unfolding on every freakin' TV in the place.

Ford had gotten home sometime around five o'clock that afternoon. As he approached his house, he saw a Volvo sitting in his driveway. His first thought was, "Not a cop car." His second thought was, "grab the crowbar anyway."

Ford suddenly recognized the man standing on his porch as the real estate agent who had rented him the house. It turned out to be just a courtesy call to ensure that all was going well with the rental. Ford knew full well that the guy was just checking to make sure that Ford had not trashed the place. Ford assured him that all was well and that he and his aged mother were very happy there.

Ford looked down at the box he had carried from the basement. It contained six pipe bombs. He had finished the last two this evening. The hard part wasn't making the bombs. The hard part had been dismantling the explosive cockpit bolts he had stolen from his old employer. Those things were a bitch to take apart and he had the bloody hands to prove it. Once the explosive had been removed from the bolts, it had to be reshaped and fitted properly into the pipe bombs.

His next chore was to fit the pipe bombs into one of the galvanized cans he had in the barn. He wanted to have one of his little surprise packages ready to go just in case tomorrow's call to the very important and beautiful people didn't go well.

...

Jake had just turned the corner and began walking along the edge of Mill Race Road. As he approached Ford's house, he did his best to stay in the shadows. Through the darkness he could make out the outline of a pickup truck. This time the pickup was parked in the street next to the mailbox. As he approached the truck, he looked up and saw that there was a light on in the kitchen. Jake stepped to the back of the truck and saw that there was a tied-down tarp covering the bed.

Jake looked up and checked the house again. He then looked up and down the street to make sure there were no headlights in the distance. When he saw no movement and no lights, he quickly untied one corner of the tarp. He bent his knees and lifted the tarp up by six inches. He stuck his arm under the tarp and turned his flashlight on for what he had planned to be two seconds.

It wasn't two seconds. It was close to ten seconds before he realized that he had to stop staring and shut his light off. "Idiot," he said to himself. He shut his light off and quickly sunk to the ground.

What he had seen in the bed of the truck was a hand cart of some kind and a round concrete slab. That, however, wasn't what caught his attention. It was the bright yellow device with the letters "CD" printed on the side. It was lying up against the round concrete slab. It had taken several seconds for Jake to realize that he was looking at a Geiger counter.

As he sat there on the ground with his back up against the rear wheel of the pickup he said to himself, "Okay, smart ass, now what?"

...

As Jake sat on the ground behind the pickup, a small fishing boat was quietly gliding up a recently built man-made inlet that fed off of Smith Creek. The men inside the boat were dressed in black. They now were busy donning black balaclavas and gloves. Each carried a Geiger counter strung from his shoulder and each carried a small Beretta, extra magazines and a flashlight in their tactical vests.

The inlet was about 30 feet wide and 200 yards long. It was lined with wooden bulkheads and tie-up cleats all along its sides. At the very end of the inlet, and set back several hundred feet from the water, a little red barn sat silhouetted against the night sky.

...

As Jake was about to stand up, he heard the sound of a screen door creaking open and then slamming shut. The noise had come from Ford's house.

Jake thought, "If he comes to his truck, I'm screwed." Jake went flat to the ground and looked under the truck. He could see a pair of legs walking across the lawn. He watched as they moved away from him and towards Betsy Vail's old house. Jake moved to the front side of the truck and peeked around the side. He could clearly see a man moving towards a building. The man was carrying what looked like a box.

The building sat back some distance from the road and was nestled in the shadows of several trees. Jake thought, "I don't remember noticing that building before." He squinted in an effort to better make out the shape of the building.

"It's a barn," he thought to himself.

He then tried to focus his eyes on the man again, but the man had disappeared.

Jake was contemplating his next move when the man suddenly appeared again and headed straight for the house.

Jake made a decision. It was a bad decision that would lead to several more bad decisions that he would make that night.

He moved from behind the truck and headed for the barn. One peek into a window was all he wanted. He would then head for his car and call on his radio for backup. He and the backup would seal the scene and he would try to wake up a Judge to get a telephonic search warrant. In light of what happened today on Asparagus Beach, he doubted that his search warrant request would be denied. Besides, if all else failed there were always FBI Agent Morse and his fed friends. Jake knew there was going to be a problem with the lawyers when it came to him peeking under the tarp covering the bed of the pickup. He also knew that regardless of how many radiation bombs there were, the lawyers would go absolutely apoplectic if they knew he had peeked into a window. He decided he would work all that out later.

Jake, staying in the shadows, began to circle the barn. He found that every window was closed with a storm shutter. Frustrated, Jake said to himself. "See, the whole freakin' window-peeking thing just solved itself." As he moved around the barn, he saw that its large front double doors had been padlocked shut. When he had almost circled the entire barn, he finally spotted a side door. It was open.

Jake could see an odd glow coming from the interior of the barn. He turned to look at Ford's house. He saw no movement and he heard no sound. It occurred to him at that very moment that perhaps Jillian Stark had been right and that he was, in fact, an asshole.

"Screw it," Jake said as he stepped through the doorway.

The first thing Jake saw when he entered the barn was seven brand new galvanized trash cans all lined up against one of the walls. As Jake's eyes scanned the open space around him, he saw the source of the odd glow. It was an old-fashioned oil lamp burning in the far corner of the barn. His eyes finally rested on what looked like an old rusted commercial van. The light was too poor to make out any of the writing on the panels and doors. But one of the doors looked like it had a big bell painted on the side.

Both the back doors to the van were open. Jake stepped up to the back bumper and pulled his flashlight from his pocket.

"Two seconds this time," he told himself.

The powerful light beam completely lit up in inside of the van. There, up against the back wall that separated the cab from the cargo area, sat seven concrete casts.

The light suddenly changed from white to a blinding white heat. This was instantly followed by a pain so intense that it buckled Jake at his knees. By the time he hit the floor, he knew that he had been struck from behind. He tried to raise his body at his knees and reach for his Glock at the same time. Then a second blow came. It missed his skull by a fraction of an inch, tore his right ear in half and fractured his collar bone.

Jake fell back to the floor and rolled onto his back. There was no hope now of drawing his Glock. The entire right side of his body was now ablaze in pain. Jake could see his attacker's face looming above him and shining in the lamp light. It was Jack Ford.

Ford held a bloody crowbar high over his head. As Ford was about to bring the crowbar down onto Jake's head for one final killing blow, he shouted, "Bye-bye, motherfucker."

His words were followed by a strange popping noise.

Jake raised his left arm up in a final feeble attempt to defend himself and waited for the final strike.

But the strike didn't come. Ford just stood there with the crowbar held high over his head and his eyes boring into Jake's.

Then a small rivulet of blood appeared in the left nostril of Ford's nose. A second later another rivulet of blood appeared in his right nostril. The rivulets joined and began to flow over Ford's now quivering lips and chin.

Ford slowly sank to his knees. With the crowbar still held high over his head, he fell over and landed next to Jake.

The back of Ford's head was facing Jake and was clearly visible in the glow of the lamp light. Ford had one of those bald spots that middle-aged men tend get right at the back of their heads. In the center of that bald spot was a tiny black hole.

Jake's eyes were barely open now. The last vestiges of consciousness were about to leave him. Then he saw a man step forward from the darkness. What was left of Jake's ability to focus went directly to the silenced pistol in the man's hand. He then looked at the face. There in the light of Jake's fading consciousness stood FBI Agent Bob Morse.

As Jake lay unconscious on the barn's floor, a man dressed all in black stood over him. He had just finished applying two pressure bandages to Jake's head. The man then gathered up the remaining items from his first aid kit.

He stepped over the body of Jack Ford and slipped out the side door of the barn.

It took him just seconds to cross the few hundred feet to the little inlet at the rear of the property. He quickly jumped aboard the waiting boat and went straight to the wheel house. As he started the engine, he turned to face Bob Morse and asked, “Do we have all seven aboard? Did you count them yourself?”

“Yes, and yes, Josh. All is good,” replied Morse. He continued, “I will need to make a 911 call soon. The American policeman is badly hurt.”

Josh Gallin nodded his head and said, “You can call when we pass through the Shinnecock Inlet. Not before.”

With that Josh Gallin guided the boat into Smith Creek and pushed the throttle forward as far as it would go.

Just after 2:00 am, a 911 dispatcher received an anonymous call stating that a man with a head injury was lying in a barn located on Mill Race Road near the corner of Oak Lane in Hampton Bays.

A short time later, as EMTs were entering the little red barn on Mill Race Road, a small fishing boat was exiting the Shinnecock Inlet and entering the Atlantic Ocean.

As it passed the final lights at the ends of the three-quarter-mile-long stone jetties, the little fishing boat was joined by two Legend Class Coast Guard Cutters. The Cutter Hamilton took up a position 100 yards off the port stern of the fishing boat. The Cutter Kimball took up a similar position on the fishing boat’s starboard side.

Standing on the bridge of the Cutter Hamilton was its Captain, William Rodgers III. Standing next to Captain Rodgers was a man in his thirties dressed in a very expensive blue suit. The man in the blue suit had been sent aboard to “monitor” the situation as it unfolded during the evening. The man said little and asked little. Captain Rodgers suspected he was from the Defense Intelligence Agency or perhaps the CIA. But Rodgers had been around long enough to keep both his suspicions and speculations to himself.

Captain Rodgers had come from a long line of naval officers. His father, Captain William Rodgers Jr., had commanded a Destroyer during the Vietnam War. His grandfather, Lt. William Rodgers, had commanded the USS Cushing. The Cushing was a Navy torpedo boat and had been one of the many vessels that helped save the passengers and crew of the ill-fated RMS Republic as it sank off the coast of Nantucket Island many years ago.

Captain Rodgers knew very little about the fishing boat he was escorting. What he did know was that he received his orders directly from the Commandant of the Coast Guard and the Commandant of the US Coast Guard can only take orders during peacetime from two people in Washington DC, those two people being the Secretary of Homeland Security and the President.

As Josh Gallin steered the fishing boat towards the prearranged rendezvous point, he turned to Bob Morse and said, "It's time to clean up."

With that, a large canvas bag was spread open on the deck. The first item to go into the bag was a large cinderblock. That was followed by all of the Geiger counters and all of the Berettas that each man had carried, including the one fired by Bob Morse. The final item to go into the bag was Bob Morse's forged FBI credentials. The canvas bag was then tied closed and tossed over the side.

The moon had broken through the cloud cover and Josh Gallin could now see the freighter sitting on the southern horizon. He thought to himself, "Soon. Soon this tragic chapter of our history will be closed for good. How many have died for these glowing pieces of metal?" It was six that he knew of. One of them being an innocent child. He thought, "We never even found out what happened to Aharon Kagan and Rachel Levy. Then there were those contaminated at that beach today. It is bound to be a dozen dead people in the end."

He glanced at the Cutter gliding along beside him on his port side. "And then there were the Americans," he thought. "They had so much to lose and would look so weak in the eyes of the world if it became known that the tiny country of Israel stole their highly prized nuclear fuel right out from under their noses. It didn't matter that it happened many years ago. The US Congress would fold under the pressure like a cheap suit and billions in defense contracts would come under question or even scrutiny." He looked over his shoulder at the Cutter one more time and said out loud, "It's your own ass you're protecting, not mine."

Less than an hour later, the seven concrete casts had been loaded onto the freighter. Both of the Cutter escorts had turned north and were moving slowly away.

Josh Gallin and Bob Morse stood on the stern of the Israeli freighter and watched the little fishing boat roll up and down over the waves. Bob Morse removed a small electronic device from his pocket. He looked at Gallin and Gallin nodded. Without another word spoken Morse pressed a little white button on the device.

There was no sound, only a small puff of smoke that rose up from below the main deck of the fishing boat. As its hull began to fill with water, the fishing boat listed to its port side. Then it rolled over and slipped below the surface.

Gallin looked at Morse and said, "Operation Apollo is finally over."

Chapter 31

Back in the Big White Building

This was Jake's third day in the hospital. When he awoke two days ago the doctor treating him told him that he had a concussion, a fractured collar bone and 36 stitches holding his right ear together. They gave him one of those little plunger buttons that was attached to a morphine drip. Someone came in and took it away that morning. He was then told by the nurse that the hospital would only allow immediate family to visit him.

He had no immediate family, so he had no visitors.

Well, that wasn't quite accurate. He did have one visitor. It was David from the records room. He pretended that there was a problem with Jake's file and managed to talk his way past the nurse's station. He only stayed for a couple of minutes. He wanted to let Jake know that both he and his grandmother were thinking of him.

Things changed for the better on the fifth day. The pain had subsided and he had his first two visitors. They were Holly Gilpin and Sue Beacher.

Holly plopped down in the chair next to him and handed him a small wrapped package and a card.

She said, "The card and the gift are from everyone in the squad. Well, almost everyone. Oh, and from Sue and John Flynn too."

Jake opened the card and read out loud, "We ran a background check on your doctor. He's wanted in six states. Love and Kisses!"

Jake smiled for the first time in days. He then yelled out in pain. It seems the smile muscles and the ear muscles are somehow attached to each other.

Jake opened the wrapped package and found a big bag of Australian Licorice. Holly knew that it was Jake's favorite.

"You know I can't chew yet," he said. "It hurts the ear. But I will make sure that it goes home with me."

Sue then said, "And this is from me."

She reached under her windbreaker and pulled out paper cup, Jake yelled, "Starbucks! I love you!"

"I had to smuggle that in here past a receptionist, a security guard and a really mean-looking nurse in the hall."

As Jake took a sip of the coffee, Sue asked, "Do you feel up to talking business? We have some stuff to tell you and a few hundred questions."

Jake said, "No problem. I would rather talk to you guys than the brass and I expect the FBI to come marching through the door at any moment." He continued, "Why don't you guys pick it from the point that somebody finds me? After you bring me up to date, I'll fill you in on what happened in the barn."

"Ok, I'll start," said Holly. "First, there was a 911 anonymous caller who basically said there was a guy with a head injury in a barn on Mill Race. They gave the cross street and hung up. I've listened to the digital recording of the call at least 50 times. I can't pick anything out except for a droning noise in the background. Two EMTs arrived within six minutes of the call and found you on the floor of the barn. They found Jack Ford lying next to you with a bullet in his head. He was gone. They didn't bother working on him."

Sue jumped in and said, "By the way, it wasn't your gun."

"I know," said Jake.

Holly continued, "Uniforms showed up about one minute after the EMTs. They saw the dead guy and sealed the crime scene. EMTs saw your holstered weapon, a cop found your ID and the Duty Officer was called. Duty Officer reached out to Detective Wilson who was on call that night. Wilson then called me because I'm senior in the squad and there is no boss. That's another story. Good so far?"

Jake nodded his head and she continued, "I arrived about an hour after they hauled you out. Nobody had noticed the big box of pipe bombs before I got there and once I heard Ford's name I put it all together real fast. I called E.S. and got the old lady out of the house. She turned out to be Ford's mother. Social Services put her up in a local motel that night and she was interviewed the next day. Once the E.S. bomb guys arrived and started working, I got a prosecutor on the phone and he woke up a local court Judge. We did a telephonic warrant sometime after 4 am. E.S. checked the place for radiation and took the bombs away."

Jake asked, "Any radiation?"

Holly answered, "No, nothing. They checked the house and pickup truck too."

Holly paused and then said, "No shell casing." She paused again and said, "We found your car at the end of Oak Lane by the water. There was another car parked next to yours. It looked like another unmarked. Turned out to be a rental out of Newark Airport. It had two days to go on the rental agreement. We're hoping for video from the rental counter, but it doesn't look good. Their surveillance system has been down for a couple of weeks. We checked the car for prints, inside and out, we got nothing. Between the stuff in the basement, barn and truck, we know Ford was our guy."

Holly looked at Sue and said, "Your turn."

Sue pulled a chair from the corner of the room and sat down on the opposite side of the bed.

She began, "I only have two things. First, the bullet that I dug out of Ford's head was a .22 long rifle. There were powder burns on the skin. It looks like someone put a gun right up against the back of his head and pulled the trigger. Second, he had deep gamma burns on his internal organs just like Zabo Pruit. I don't know if he would have survived the ARS or not, but had he lived he would gone through hell."

Sue continued, "Do you want to hear about the stuff they found on Asparagus Beach?"

"Sure," said Jake.

Sue began, "Well, once they got it capped, they dug out all around the can holding the cast. They cut away the sand so that they could use a forklift to carry it over to a flatbed truck. They strapped it down and headed for Brookhaven Lab. They shut down three major highways and had the truck surrounded by cop cars the whole way. I think they were concerned about some nutcase ramming a car into the flatbed. They had two SWAT teams and two helicopters in on the escort too. It took them five hours to drive to the lab. They were met at the lab gate by the lab police, and the stuff went to a special storage facility. Here's the part I want to tell you about. The lab scientists ran a gamma spectrometer on the stuff and identified it as Cobalt-60. This is the weird part. There was so much of it. They had never even heard of that much Cobalt-60 being stored anywhere or at any time. Bottom line is this, what they now have stored out at Brookhaven Lab is what probably killed Zabo Pruit."

Jake didn't quite feel like telling his part of the story yet so he shifted the subject. "What ever happened to Lieutenant Blair and Jillian Stark?"

Holly answered, "Funny story. After the Commissioner and all the other Chiefs reviewed the video that was anonymously posted on YouTube..." Holly paused for a second and continued, "... it was referred to Internal Affairs to determine if it was real or was it just bad cop humor. A couple of interviews later, IA reports back that there was no acting involved. What you saw, is what she is. To make matters worse, one of the IA detectives coughed during the interview and didn't cover his mouth. She went into a tirade and threatened to sue him. All available on digital video of course. IA has her gun and shield pending the results of the psychological exam. The squad has been making donations to her. The last time I counted there were 33 new cans of Lysol on her desk."

Jake asked, "And the boyfriend?"

"Another funny story. It seems that the Lieutenant in charge of the Property Bureau will be retiring in 30 days. Three guesses as to who is going to replace him. In the meantime, Blair will be working out of the Chief-of-

Detectives office. I saw him doing the lunch run for them yesterday."

"One last question, then I know it's my turn to talk," said Jake. "Any leads on the Patti Ball case?"

Holly answered, "Word on the street is that it was a mob hit. He supposedly got into a physical altercation with a made guy at a Queens night club. Things got real ugly and then somebody paid him a visit. You know how things go. It could be true, it could be half true. We'll know two years from now when some wiseguy who's looking at life in a six by six room decides to vomit up all of his so-called friends."

The hospital room had gotten very quiet. Jake had closed his eyes for a moment.

Sue asked, "Jake, you want to rest now? We can come back."

Jake opened his eyes and said, "No, let's start."

Holly pulled out her notebook and began to take notes.

"After I got your call, Holly, I got a hit on one of the plates I had photographed on Mill Race a few days before. It came back to Ford. I figured I would check out the house. I parked down by the water and walked back to Mill Race. I saw someone moving between the house and the barn and then back again. I decided to take a look in the barn."

Holly stopped writing, raised an eyebrow and said, "Bold move."

"Stupid move," Jake said in a soft voice. Jake paused for a second and said, "Jillian Stark might not be all that crazy."

Holly said, "Jake, forget about what that bag of nuts had to say. Finish your story."

Jake said, "I went into the barn, saw some cans against a wall and the old van. The back doors to the van were open but there wasn't enough light to see anything. I turned on my flashlight and saw the casts."

Holly jumped in, "Casts, what casts?"

Jake said, "The seven concrete casts that were lined up in front of the cargo area, up by the cab."

Holly said, "Jake, there was nothing in the van. I went over the inside of the thing inch-by-inch. There was nothing."

Jake said, "The FBI must have taken them."

Holly said, "Jake, you're not making any sense. Just continue your story. We can come back to this part later."

Jake continued, "I had my light on for two seconds when I got hit from behind. I fell and got hit again. I think that was the one that took out my ear and collarbone. I was on my back. I couldn't use my right arm and that's when I saw Ford coming at me with a crowbar. He had it high over his head. I think he called me a motherfucker. All of a sudden he stopped moving and talking and just fell over. That's when I saw Agent Morse standing right behind where Ford had been standing."

Holly interrupted, "Wait a minute, are you saying that Morse shot Ford in the back of the head?"

Jake said, "I know what I saw. Morse had a gun in his hand. It had a silencer on it. Then I went to sleep and woke up in this bed. That's it."

No one spoke for a full minute.

Finally Sue spoke and said, "Holy crap!"

Holly put her pen down and said, "That's what you think? You think that the feds took the casts, because you saw Morse in the barn?"

Jake nodded his head up and down.

Holly looked at Sue and said, "Sue, would you mind going down to the lunch counter and getting me a cup of coffee. I just have a couple of questions left for Jake."

Sue had been working around cops long enough to know that Holly didn't want her to hear the next part of the conversation. Sue got up from her chair and said, "Sure," and left the room.

Holly turned to Jake and said, "There is something else, Jake. It looks like there is no Bob Morse from the FBI."

Jake said, "What? No, No, No. I called their hot line and he tried to call me back. Then he showed up at my house. I even saw his …" Jake stopped talking. The image of Morse standing over Ford's dead body and holding a silenced .22 caliber pistol suddenly popped into his head.

Jake asked, "Holly, what the hell is going on?"

She answered, "I don't know. But you weren't the only one fooled. Chris Hall in Intelligence actually emailed a copy of Ford's letter to him. Morse was good, whoever he was."

Epilogue

Jake Tucker sat at his teak desk in his dining room sipping away at his coffee. It was early evening and he was enjoying his view of the bay. He was listening, as he liked to do, to the sound of the ocean waves pounding onto Ponquogue Beach. It had been seven days since he arrived home from the hospital. Most of the bandages had come off and the stitches were due to come out any day now. If things went well, he would be back at work next week.

He was now having one of those conversations with himself. The kind of conversation where you ask yourself what the hell you are doing. In the last two years he had been stabbed, shot and beaten with a crowbar. He knew guys that had been on the job for 30 years and never gotten so much as a splinter. How the hell did Jack Ford sneak up on me like that? he wondered. And why am I sitting here alone?

His mind drifted and the image of Jillian Stark popped into his head. He had hoped he had seen and heard the last from her. No such luck though. He had gotten a call from the legal department today and some department lawyer told him that he had been named in a gender discrimination lawsuit filed by you-know-who.

Just as Jake finished the last of his coffee there was a knock at his door. As he got up from his desk he thought about the last person who had knocked on his door. It was that phony FBI agent. Jake grabbed his Glock from the kitchen counter and went to the door.

As he swung the door open and looked out, he said out loud, "You have got to be kidding me." There were three of them. All of them with their FBI credentials in their hands.

Jake thought quickly, "I've been down this road before." Each one of them wore a very expensive grey suit and the only way you could tell them apart was by the color of their ties. That included the female agent. As it turned out, none of them were from the New York FBI Office or the Joint

Terrorism Task Force. All three were from FBI headquarters in Washington D.C. The leader of the pack introduced himself as Wayne something or other. He then introduced the other two, but Jake had stopped listening. Wayne started the conversation off by saying, "Detective Tucker, we tried to call your cell phone but there was no answer."

Jake said, "My phone is dead. I dropped it into a fine Italian roast and it died."

Wayne ignored Jake's comment and said, "We talked to your colleague Detective Gilpin and she was kind enough to share her reports regarding the Jack Ford case." Since Jake hadn't heard a question yet he decided to remain silent. Wayne seemed to squirm a little and then continued, "Well, we were wondering if you could shed some light on the seven concrete casts you saw in the van in the barn?"

This was followed by more silence and Jake said, "Sure, ask me any question you want."

Wayne then asked, "Okay, did you see any markings on the casts?"

"No," said Jake rather curtly.

The female agent clearly didn't like the tone of Jake's answer and chimed in, "Because there was no marking or because you didn't look?"

Jake's eyes shifted to the female agent and said, "It was because my professional observations were rudely interrupted by a man who repeatedly hit me in the head with a tire iron. He's dead now."

Wayne jumped in quickly and said, "We are sorry for your injuries, Detective, and we know it was a difficult night for you. We are just trying to obtain some information." He continued, "Detective Tucker, do you have any idea what happened to those seven casts?"

"Sure," replied Jake. "You people took them."

All three of the agents exchanged quick glances and then Wayne said, "If you're referring to the man named Bob Morse, he did not work for the Bureau."

Jake snapped back, "Of course he worked for the Bureau. How else could I call an FBI phone number in New York and have someone return my call and leave messages for me thirty minutes later, unless that person worked for the Bureau? If I remember correctly, the same thing happened to Detective Hall over in our Intelligence Section. Unless of course you're suggesting that someone managed to tap into all of your phones and computer systems?"

Jake looked from one agent to the next and said, "Tell me, guys, which sounds more plausible to you? Bob Morse was a real agent or someone tapped into the FBI communications and stole information? If you choose the former, and by the way that's my top choice, then you people have the casts. If it's the latter, your precious Bureau is in serious trouble." Jake paused, took a breath and asked, "Are we done here?"

Parked on Lighthouse Road, about one hundred feet down from Jake's house, a lone figure watched as three people left his house and got into an official-looking sedan. Once the sedan's tail lights had disappeared into the distant darkness, the lone figure got out of the car and headed for Jake's door. A great deal of worry and planning had gone into this moment. There would be just this one chance.

Jake had just finished rinsing out his coffee cup when there was another knock at his door. "Damn!" Jake said out loud. "And they wonder why local cops don't like them." Jake left his Glock on the kitchen counter this time. He went straight to the door and wrenched it open. There, standing before him, was Elizabeth Quinn. It was a full minute before either one of them spoke. It was Elizabeth who spoke the first words.

She said, "I think I have found the RMS Republic's gold." She then marched straight past him into the house. Jake closed the door behind her and followed her into the kitchen.

The End

AUTHOR'S NOTES

As is the case with most historical fiction stories, I have attempted to take actual facts, circumstances and characters from the past and have blended them into a fictional story. In this instance, the 1965 theft of over 200 pounds of Highly Enriched Uranium from the NUMEC plant in Apollo Pennsylvania was quite real. The theft has been referred to in many texts as the "*Apollo Affair*" and in 1976 the CIA reported to the Nuclear Regulatory Commission that they believed the missing Highly Enriched Uranium went to Israel.

The serial killer David Berkowitz, also known as the '*Son of Sam,"* terrorized the streets of New York City for over a year. Berkowitz had been adopted at an early age and his true name was Richard Falco. In the end, he murdered 6 people and wounded 7 others. This particular case has played on my conscience for over 40 years. During Berkowitz's reign of terror, I was a police officer in New York City and on March 8, 1977, I came very close to meeting this madman on the streets of Forest Hills. At 6:45 pm on that very evening, I had parked my 1973 Chevy Camaro on Continental Avenue under the Long Island Rail Road trestle. I had visited the Tobacconist shop before heading to my apartment several blocks away. Forty-five minutes later, at 7:30 pm, Berkowitz shot and killed 21-year-old Virginia Voskerichian just a few yards away from where I had been parked on Continental Avenue.

David Berkowitz's desire to commit mass murder on Asparagus Beach in Amagansett came to light during his 50 hours of prison interviews with forensic psychiatrist David Abrahamsen. According to Dr. Abrahamsen's notes, Berkowitz indicated that he had visited the beach at the end of Atlantic Avenue as a child with his adoptive parents. He also indicated that he had intended on using a machine gun to commit mass murder on that very beach in August of 1977.

Berkowitz had stated to Dr. Abrahamsen that the only thing that prevented him from carrying out his plan on that August evening was the fact that it had begun to rain. David Berkowitz drove a 1970 yellow Ford Galaxie and a .45 caliber machine gun was found in his car at the time of his arrest.

During my research for this book I found it to be a truly amazing coincidence that Nazi saboteurs had landed on the very beach that Berkowitz had chosen to commit his mass murder. This failed German intelligence and sabotage mission was part of a larger plan called *"Operation Pastorius"* and involved numerous German submarine landings along the U.S. coast line during World War II. In the end, all of the saboteurs were caught by the FBI. Two of the eight saboteurs received lengthy prison sentences. The remaining six saboteurs were executed by electrocution on August 8, 1943, on the third floor of the city's jail in Washington D.C.

Many of the anecdotal stories told throughout the book are true. In particular, the nuclear reactor explosion at the SL-1 site in Idaho Falls, Idaho in 1961 and the 1987 release of Cesium-137 in Goiânia, Brazil, are still used today as models for emergency responder training throughout the United States. In addition, "young Johnny's" little incident with the glow stick did, in fact, occur at the Suffolk County Police Department's 3rd Precinct. I was there. It was a long night.

In 1996, an individual by the name of John J. Ford was arrested and charged with scheming to kill the chairman of the Suffolk County Republican Party, a Suffolk legislator, a leader of the Conservative Party and the chief investigator in a local Town Attorney's office. He and one of his accomplices, Edward Zabo, were planning on introducing radium into their victim's cars and lacing their toothpaste with radioactive metal.

The subsequent criminal investigation determined that Mr. Ford wanted these officials killed because he believed they were interfering with his efforts to contact aliens from outer space. Mr. Ford's friends said he believed that visitors from outer space had crash-landed on Long Island and that government officials were keeping the aliens at Brookhaven National Laboratory in Upton and that they had created diversionary fires in Long Island's Pine Barrens to conceal the aliens' crash landings. A Suffolk County Court judge concluded that Mr. Ford was delusional and unfit to stand trial.

The day of Edward Zabo's arrest, a RAP team from Brookhaven National Laboratory, Emergency Service Officers from the SCPD, and I searched his home and found thousands of hand tools, explosives and radioactive materials. At the time of his arrest, Edward Zabo was carrying a briefcase. The briefcase's only contents were a single ballpeen hammer.

Finally, it is important to know that there is a small man-made inlet leading directly off of Smith Creek in Hampton Bays. At the end of that inlet, set back just a few hundred feet from the water's edge, stands a little red barn.

ABOUT THE AUTHOR

Steven C. Drielak is an internationally recognized expert in the area of Hot Zone Forensic Attribution. He received his Master's degrees from John Jay College of Criminal Justice in New York City. He has over 30 years of law enforcement experience. Steven was responsible for the establishment of the Suffolk County Environmental Crime Unit in New York and commanded that unit for 16 years. Steven has served as a Director within the EPA's Office of Criminal Enforcement, Forensics and Training in both the Homeland Security and Criminal Enforcement national programs. As the Director of the EPA's *National Criminal Enforcement Response Team* he was responsible for deploying environmental forensic evidence collection teams to BP Alaska's Prudhoe Bay oil pipeline failures, the BP Deepwater Horizon incident and the West Texas Fertilizer Company explosion.

Steven has served as a senior forensic attribution instructor and program developer for the Department of Homeland Security's, Federal Law Enforcement Training Center in Glynco, GA and had served for 17 years as a National Academy Instructor for the EPA's criminal enforcement program. He has also provided environmental forensic attribution training for the FBI's *Hazardous Materials Response Unit*. He has also provided international training to numerous countries within the European Union. He has authored and co-authored 5 text books in the areas of Environmental Crimes, Weapons of Mass Destruction and Forensic Attribution. He has served as an appointed member of the International Association of Chiefs of Police *Environmental Crimes Committee* and had served on the President's *Interagency Microbial Forensics Advisory Board*.

Made in the USA
Middletown, DE
14 March 2019